CAPTAIN ZERO:
THE GOLDEN MURDER SYNDICATE

THE GOLDEN MURDER
SYNDICATE

By G. T. Fleming–Roberts

STEEGER BOOKS • 2020

PUBLISHING HISTORY

"The Golden Murder Syndicate" originally appeared in the March 1950 (Vol. 1, No. 3) issue of *Captain Zero* magazine. Copyright © 1950 by Popular Publications, Inc. Copyright renewed © 1978 and assigned to Steeger Properties, LLC. All rights reserved.

CHAPTER 1
SOUND THE HOUR
OF MURDER!

"I'M AFRAID."

She hadn't intended to speak aloud. That had slipped out. Now, on the fringe of the crowd at the Crystal Dance Palace, she darted a glance about to see if anyone had heard. No one had. She was ten feet from the nearest slowly swaying couple. Twenty feet from the velvet rope behind which the stagline straggled. She was alone, and she meant to stay that way, to keep beyond *his* reach. Beyond his firm, possessive touch and the appraising stare of his dark eyes.

She had told him she was going to the powder room. Now she hesitated, her evening purse clutched in her small, white-knuckled fists, and looked for him across the room. He was standing near the main exit. Near the alcove where he'd checked her light evening wrap. He was a slight man in a creamy tan suit with a deep brown shirt and a pale tan tie. Too sharp, she thought. She ought to have known what he was from the way he dressed. She *must* have known but had skipped the apprehensive present to reach the future.

She'd seen him across the threshold of her furnished room, and her mind had plunged enthusiastically on to tomorrow. Here was her first feature article, she'd thought. She'd show that doubting Thomas of a managing editor at the *Daily World*.

All evening she'd thought about tomorrow. Smiling at him,

her mind strung words together: *Miss Prudence shows imprudence in selection of escorts for lonely girls. Feature writer blind-dates an eye-opener.*

Stealthily, though, the present had crept up on her. It had prodded her with a cold hard lump that she'd discovered beneath her escort's double-breasted jacket when she'd danced with him. A gun? All this and a gun too?

A gun and a pair of eyes. They had no depth, those eyes of his. Only surface, the pupils contracted to mere pin-points. They were dark mirrors into which she had looked and seen herself, her forced smile drooping.

My God, she'd thought, he's a drug addict!

Well, to heck with the story. Let somebody else hold the mirror up to life. And to heck with my wrap. What's twenty dollars? He's standing there because he thinks I won't leave without my wrap. He knows, somehow, that I intend to give him the slip, and he thinks he's got me blocked.

She turned, moved past the door of the powder room. Her high heels broke rhythm with *Some Enchanted Evening*. It was enchanted, all right. It was hexed. A dope fiend with a gun! But she mustn't run and she mustn't look back. She mustn't do anything that might attract his attention. She mustn't even think of him.

She walked on and glanced casually through one of the white plaster arches that opened from the rim of the ballroom. There was a pool and a tiny fountain, a lovers' nook complete with lovers. Nice clean kids, drinking cokes, starry-eyed over one another. This was a nice place, the Crystal Palace, approved by parents and the City Fathers. Approved, no doubt, by the fire marshal, she thought as she thrust against the panic lock on a door beneath a red illuminated sign.

As she descended the stairs, wilting heat washed over her, but that was better than the air conditioning to which *his* presence had lent a distinct clamminess. A sign painted on the stairwell wall reminded her: *Don't Run. This Stair Is Fireproof.* No, don't run. Walk sedately as though you always leave a ballroom by the back stairs and alone. Someday you'll laugh at this. Tomorrow, maybe.

TOMORROW. TOMORROW was a lump of disappointment in her throat. She'd be on the bus, going back to Rosedale. She'd washed out. She'd have to confess that to the folks. She'd have to admit she wasn't cut out for journalism. What had happened to change her mind? Well, nothing had actually happened.

I'm gutless, she thought guiltily and paused halfway down a stair flight, one hand gripping the rail. She glanced down at her hand, at the rail itself. The rail was a thick black pipe. The rail had changed. It was pipe and not smooth polished wood on bronze supports as it had been on the other flights. She'd gone too far down. She'd missed the ground floor and was on her way into the basement. Suppose he followed her into the basement, into some dead-end pocket in the boiler room?

She turned and ran confusedly up to the next landing. There was a door, another panic lock. Well-named, panic lock, she thought as she pushed her way into a short brilliantly lighted hall where there was a door that carried the legend: TO PEARL sᴛ. She took her first deep, satisfying breath and headed for that door. Now she was all right. Now she was away from him.

She stood for a moment outside the building and tried to get her bearings. She was in a narrow alley that seemed remote from the brilliantly illuminated marquee of the theater and ballroom beneath which she and her escort had passed to enter the building.

There was a single bug-swirled light above her and beyond its feeble reaches the canyon of dark stretched in either direction. She turned to the left, took perhaps ten steps before she came to a faltering stop. Strength trickled out of her legs like sand from a bag. Her mouth was open and dry and soundless.

"You forgot your wrap," he said.

He was wraithlike in the gloom—so thin, his light tan suit, her white wrap over his arm.

"You forgot your wrap," he repeated, stepping to her side.

"Th-thanks." How utterly inane that sounded. "I—I felt suddenly sick—" His thin strong fingers on her arm, and her flesh crept.

"Then I'll take you home," he said.

"Please— No, I'll take a cab—"

"I said I'd take you home."

They were walking now, his hand locked on her wrist, her forearm against his and pressed against his lean ribs.

"No," she protested faintly, "it isn't right." She forced a laugh. "I—this headache of mine—it's spoiled your evening. You go back to the ballroom, why don't you? Find some other girl—"

"Baby, I like you," he said. "I go for you in a big way."

"No, you don't. You don't even know me. I'm not your type at all."

"You're my type exactly," he said.

THEY'D TURNED into a cove at the rear of two buildings, and she saw the parking lot. It was dimly illuminated and deserted. She saw his car among the others, an old Lincoln as black as a hearse.

"You're my type," he was saying. "I looked through all the pix that old cat had and saw yours and said, 'That's for me.' You, baby. I like everything about you."

"D-d-don't hold my arm so tight."

He didn't say anything. He opened the left hand door of the Lincoln without relinquishing his hold upon her arm. She thought, As soon as he hands me in and starts around to the other side, I'll jump out and run. I'll run and scream for help.

But then he wasn't handing her into the car. He got in first and kept his hold upon her wrist. He dragged her up onto the cushion beside him. He reached across her, got the door handle, slammed the door. And then, very carefully, like balancing an egg on end, he let go of her arm to turn the ignition switch.

Her right hand inched along her thigh, lifted to the door panel, crept toward the handle. He had the engine started now and was occupied with shifting gears. Her grip tightened on the handle. Her arm tensed. A quick wrench and she'd have the door open. She'd spring out and run for it.

She knew where she was now, and she could reach the street. There'd be someone there to help her, she was sure. But when she tried to turn the handle it wouldn't budge. It was locked some way, or he'd jammed it. A thin cry of dismay escaped her lips, and his hand flicked from the gear shift lever and onto her face—a sharp, back-handed blow across the mouth that rocked her head back against the cushions.

"Try that again, baby, and I'll break your sweet neck," he said without the faintest trace of emotion.

As the car started to roll across the lot, she forced herself to go limp, to sink deep into the cushions. She squeezed her eyelids tight shut against the stinging tears.

"I won't try anything," she said, her voice faint, submissive. "I'll be good. I promise."

"That's more like it," he said and rammed his foot down on the accelerator.

She kept her eyes closed. Her body was as limp as a rag doll. Somewhere, above the high whine of the transmission, a steeple bell tolled the hour. She counted the strokes. Nine. Ten. Eleven. Twelve. Midnight. This was tomorrow. Dark tomorrow.

WHEN THE little French clock on the false mantel in her Broadmoor Avenue apartment chimed the first stroke of midnight, Miss Ada Franzer dog-eared the page of her library book, put the top on the box of chocolates she had bought for herself, and stood up. She was fifty-five, comfortably plump and ungirdled, and her only reason for fulfilling life's little routines on unvarying schedule was that she had found that it simplified everything. Therefore, regardless of how interesting her novel might be, she closed it at midnight and went to bed where she would remain until precisely eight o'clock in the morning.

This was Sunday night which meant that she would have to

wind the clock. She crossed the living room which she would have described as "uncluttered" without realizing that it was actually as sterile as her own selfish and maidenly existence. She fingered the brass key from beneath the clock, opened the crystal in order to fit the key into the proper place.

"My Basil, you *are* run down," she said to the clock and laughed quietly at her own joke. She'd christened the clock Basil after the ardent admirer who had given it to her over thirty years ago and who had sworn to kill himself if she didn't marry him.

It had proved an empty oath, however, for the last she had heard of Basil-the-man he had five children, a wife in the hospital with gallstones, and Miss Franzer congratulated herself on sticking to her resolution to live alone and like it.

When Basil-the-clock was, as she put it, "tight," Miss Franzer entered the bedroom and approached the east casement to lower the awning against tomorrow's sun. This, also, was a part of her schedule, a chore that had to be performed before she disrobed.

She unlatched the screen, pulled it toward her and, before groping around the edge of the window frame for the awning cord, planted her feet firmly on the floor. She had a fear of height, the awning was heavy, and she braced herself against the truly fantastic idea that the awning cord might jerk her out through the window.

The awning was half lowered when she heard the burst of gunfire in old Duncan Moore's apartment which occupied the entire floor above—five or six shots tumbling one over the other to blend into a single and continuous roar. The awning cord burned through Miss Franzer's fingers and slapped out into the dark. She dropped back from the window, stood with the back of her left hand plastered over her open mouth, wall-eyed with terror.

"My gracious!" she said when she could say anything at all. "Mr. Moore! He must have—" She let that go because the idea that Mr. Moore had killed himself seemed hardly feasible. Too many shots. One would certainly have accomplished the suicide of an old man confined to a wheeled chair.

Miss Franzer's next notion pictured Mr. Moore and that heathenish looking houseboy of his, fighting a duel. Why, then, the utter silence? She listened eagerly a moment for the pelting of footsteps and the slamming of doors. There was nothing of the sort either on the floor above nor on her floor. She remembered that the Evanses—her neighbors on the north—had gone out for the evening and that the Clarks were in Maine for the summer.

Miss Franzer's fear became a very personal thing as she realized that it was quite possible that she and she alone had heard the shots. Some thoughtless murderer had thus foisted upon Miss Ada Franzer the undesired responsibility of doing something about whatever had happened on the floor above.

"Oh, dammit!" said Miss Franzer. Still pop-eyed, she groped to the bed and sat on the edge of it. The midnight silence was all-prevading. She had a good mind just to go to bed and forget the whole thing.

"Except that I wouldn't sleep," she said. "Not with murderers about." And, she added mentally, I'm not a very good liar either, and they'd certainly want to know why I didn't hear the shots. "I've got to do my duty as a citizen," she decided aloud.

She stood, took determined steps into the living room where the 'phone was. Finger on the dial, she glanced about her ivory tower and pictured it as it would probably be in a very short while.

"Full of men with hats on," she said contemptuously. "Slumping in my chairs, scattering cigar ashes about. Police? Pah!" She sighed deeply, lifted the 'phone, and dialed "O" for the operator.

"How in the world does one go about calling the police?" Miss Franzer asked the operator bewilderedly. "I think there's something wrong upstairs."

AT MIDNIGHT by his watch, Ned Bardon pronged the telephone handset on the side of the coin box and stepped through the open door of the booth in Melton's Bowling Alley on the south side of town. He crossed in front of the nearly deserted spectators' gallery behind the foul lines, paused to watch a girl in a bright yellow T-shirt make a strike, then moved unhurriedly to the big semi-circular counter where a red-haired man wearing blue wash pants and a white undershirt was gouging at the bowl of his pipe with a knife.

The redhead looked up and Ned Bardon smiled, nodded. "Joe," he said.

"How're they goin'?" Joe asked without interest. There was only a faint glimmer of recognition in his blue eyes.

Ned Bardon hung his left hip on the counter. "How's everything, Joe?"

" 'S too damned hot." Joe closed the knife against his thigh and shook his head to decline the cigarettes the tall blond man offered. "I stick to my pipe."

"I remember." Ned Bardon took a silver cigarette lighter out of the pocket of his gray gabardine trousers. "I thought maybe I'd find Murph around here tonight."

"Huh uh." Joe frowned. "The big Irish. I don't see much of him since—" He broke off as recognition dawned. "Now I make you," he said, and his voice lost its trace of cordiality. "Soon as you mention the big Irish, I knew who you was. Bardon. I get forgetful in my old age."

Ned Bardon had a slow smile that showed bright, rather large teeth. "Murph and I used to bowl here twice a week right after we got out of the Army. How is Murph, anyway?"

"The same," Joe said. His eyes carefully appraised Ned Bardon's expensive clothes. "He don't change," Joe added as though to imply that some people did. "Murph said you got yourself a swell job, that you're going up."

"Speaking of my job, is that clock right?"

Joe glanced over his shoulder at the electric clock on the wall. "Ask Western Union. I close when they get tired of knocking 'em over."

The clock hands stood at one minute after midnight. Ned Bardon lighted his cigarette and slid off the counter. He was tall and lean. In the fluorescent light his fair skin looked thin and waxy.

"Be seeing you, Joe," Ned Bardon said in his easy, offhand manner.

Joe didn't say anything.

A girl stood on the sidewalk somewhat to the left of the entrance of the bowling alley. She'd been standing there for quite some time without moving except to shift her weight from one foot to the other or to tug self-consciously at her black, too-tight, too-short skirt. One of her stockings had a conspicuous run. The toes of her black patent leather pumps were crisscrossed with gray cracks. She had a full-lipped, sullen mouth and odd, darkly brooding eyes.

WHEN NED BARDON stepped out of the door, the girl stiffened perceptibly. Her indrawn breath was sharply audible, yet he didn't notice, didn't turn to look at her at all. As he moved off to the east, the girl's right hand lifted, fluttered in a staying gesture. Eyes momentarily closed, she swayed slightly forward before she caught her balance. Then, lower lip in her teeth, she watched him disappear.

Her eyes were hot and bright.

Jessop Street, in this block, was a tight little bottleneck, and yellow paint on the curbs on either side prohibited parking. Light from the bowling alley entrance peeled away from Ned Bardon and left him a feeling of nakedness. The night was hot and sullen and still, and Ned Bardon caught himself tiptoeing across it, hurrying a little to get into the island of light from the corner street lamp.

Then he was all right. His footsteps rang. As long as the light lasted, they rang, and he breathed deep and free. But with the light at his back, he again knew uneasiness. Cars crowded the curb on one hand while on the other, the dark, squalid dwellings seemed to inch a little nearer the sidewalk with every step he took. His own car was parked at the end of the block, but there was no street light there—only the seeming infinity of the night.

Ned Bardon stopped. Somewhere ahead of him, a car door opened. Shadows emerged, black against black. There was a brief scuffling sound. A man laughed shortly. A woman's scream was stifled before it was well begun.

Ned Bardon stood where he was. Lovers' quarrel, the preliminaries to a wife beating—he didn't know what it was, and he didn't give a good damn. He just didn't want to get mixed up in it, that was all.

The girl broke away. She came racing along the sidewalk, toward the light. Toward Ned Bardon standing tall against the light. He couldn't see her. She was any woman running—the *skish-skish* of thin soles on concrete, the whip of her skirts. And the man behind her was any man.

"Help me, for God's sake!"

She sobbed that at Ned Bardon as she caught his left arm and swung herself around behind him. Then he was mixed up in it. But good. He was sandwiched between the two of them, the girl clutching him from behind, sawing on his arms, the man's breath in his face.

Ned Bardon had barely time to break the girl's hold on him before the man delivered a blow that struck his shoulder and rocked him. Ned Bardon feinted with his right and shot his left. He'd always had a good left. This one was perfect. It landed with a satisfying and solid sound in the middle of somebody's face. And that, unaccountably, was that. The somebody went down all at once like a house built of toy blocks. He stayed down. There was not the slightest stir of sound that might indicate he cared to get up again.

Ned Bardon took a breath. "All right—" he began but broke off to glance over his left shoulder. The woman had kept on running. She was beyond the intersection now, the light at her back. She could have been blond or brunette. She could, for that matter, have been Chinese. The only thing that was definite about her was that she was gone. The dark had swallowed her.

Ned Bardon put out a cautious foot and touched the man on the sidewalk. The man didn't complain. He didn't do anything.

"Hey, you!" Anxiety crept into Ned Bardon's voice. He shoved a hand down into a trouser pocket and brought out his lighter. He knelt. His left hand found a shoulder and shook it, while his right fumbled the lighter open and thumbed the spark wheel.

The wick caught and the flickering light revealed a slight man dressed in a light tan suit and a dark brown shirt. He lay on his back, legs wide-spread, shoulders and head elevated slightly by a squat red fireplug. His face was thin, knobby, and with his dark eyes open, protruding, and slightly crossed, he looked stupid.

Also, he looked dead.

Ned Bardon stared bewilderedly for a moment at the man's face, at the red wetness that crawled down the thick, fluted column of the fireplug. He snapped the lighter shut, stood, stumbled over the sprawled legs, looked back and down once more.

"My God," he whispered hoarsely. And then he broke into a run toward his car.

TWO BLOCKS north of Jessop Street, in a furnished room

on the second floor of a lodging house, a young man sat limply in a chair and stroked the long black ears of a huge, part-Newfoundland dog. He was a small man, slight, with colorless features and thick-lensed, horn-rimmed glasses.

It was then not yet midnight, but no one in the city of Pendleville could have been more keenly aware of the fleeting minutes than Lee Allyn. Every little while he would look at his watch. Then he would hold his hand up to the light of the bridge lamp that stood beside his chair, and study the natural pink aura of translucency about his fingertips.

At seven minutes before twelve, the translucent area had increased perceptibly. Lee Allyn stooped, untied the laces of his oxfords and removed them. He replaced rayon socks with rawhide soled woolen boot-liners. He stripped off his outer garments and appeared in tight-fitting white wool shorts and T-shirt. Lastly, he traded his horn-rimmed glasses for a pair of invisible contact lenses ground for the same correction.

Eleven fifty-eight by Lee Allyn's watch. The eyes of the huge black dog watching him expectantly, Allyn crossed the room to the chest of drawers on top of which he found a scrap of paper which carried the penciled name "Schoenling" together with a Jessop Street address.

As he crumpled the bit of paper to toss it into the wastebasket, Lee Allyn noticed that the bones of his hands were now clearly silhouetted against the light as though his flesh had been penetrated by X-rays. Nor was the phenomenal effect confined to his hands alone. Every portion of his body seemed gradually to melt from view. His face was literally the merest shadow of itself, the shadow dissolving into twilight gray that grew ever thinner until it had vanished utterly.

And then the amazing rays that emanated from within his body began to permeate the animal fibers of his tight-fitting, scanty garments until they too were perfectly transparent. None but the keenest observer would have been aware that the room was occupied by a living creature other than the big black dog.

The dog stretched, then stood alertly, its great plume of a tail wagging, its eyes expectant.

"Not tonight, Blackie," the voice of the unseen man spoke.

The dog's ears dropped, its eyes saddened. It crouched on the floor and followed its unseen master's footsteps with keen ears. The door of the room was quietly opened by an invisible hand, and then as quietly closed. The dog sighed, rested its muzzle on its forelegs, and closed its eyes.

Captain Zero had left the house.

CHAPTER 2
THE BIG FRAME

IT WAS not until Ned Bardon was putting his car into the garage back of his own apartment building that he thought, What a damned fool thing to do, to run out on a thing like that! I ought to have gone back to the bowling alley and called the cops. That was the logical, the sane thing to do. I must be nuts!

Still, there was the woman. Or rather, there wasn't the woman. That was what had thrown him off balance—her running out on him like that.

17

Suppose, he thought as he entered the building through the alley door, just suppose she takes it into her head to stay out of the whole mess? Suppose the cops finally get around to me, and I can't produce any woman. And I can't, that's for sure, because I don't know a thing about her.

He went up the stairs and along the second floor corridor. His keys tangled nervously as he unlocked the door of his flat. He got the door open and switched on the lamps, aware suddenly of a familiar and delicate perfume that hung in the air. It was a big living room, comfortably, tastefully furnished, and he ordinarily became conscious of a sense of satisfaction whenever he stepped into it. Not tonight. He felt trapped.

He crossed to the broad window overlooking Piedmont Street, opened it. For a moment, he stood there and listened to the night—the chirp of insects in the foreground, the distinct rush of traffic on Broadmoor Avenue. Heat came into the room and settled itself on Ned Bardon.

He lit a cigarette, told himself that what he needed was a good stiff drink. He drank only in moderation, for when you were employed by a staid old investment house like Earhart & Cline you had to be moderate in everything. But now he really needed a drink.

He turned from the window, started toward the kitchenette, paused at a record cabinet on top of which was a wireless record player. There was a seven inch white wax-covered disk on the turntable. Ned Bardon nipped his cigarette in his lips and, squinting against the smoke, picked the disk off the turntable only to let it fall back onto the spindle from nervous fingers as somebody knocked at the door of the apartment.

He stood motionless and without breathing, stared at the door out of the corner of his eye. His face had a tense, drawn look about it. The knock was repeated. He took a slow deep breath and crossed to the door.

THE MAN beyond the threshold was enormously fat. The white linen suit that partially contained him was wrinkled where it was not stretched beyond its capacity. His face sagged out of a Panama hat, and a terrace of chins overran the collar of his sweat-dappled white shirt.

A short snipe of a cigar defined his mouth which might otherwise have gone unnoticed among the rest of the convolutions and creases. Something approaching a smile crinkled the corners of small black eyes, and he put out a huge right hand to Ned Bardon while its mate remained in the sagging pocket of his jacket.

"Mr. Bardon, I haven't the slightest doubt," he said. "The name is Schoenling, Paul Schoenling." And he chuckled.

"Is that supposed to be funny?" Bardon asked coldly. He didn't take the hand. It took him by the forearm so that, as he drew instinctively back, he towed the fat man into the room.

"Funny? No, I don't suppose so. Not at this hour of the night, I don't suppose it's funny at all. And you're quite right, Mr. Bardon—that hard object prodding you in my left pocket *is* a gun. A small but efficient persuader." He chuckled happily. "I *am* ambidextrous. So if you have any notion of ejecting me forcibly from this charming flat, think about it twice, my dear fellow."

Schoenling had by this time backed Ned Bardon a couple of paces from the door. The fat man now turned with surprising speed and closed the door. He wheeled, smiling, and nodded at a chair.

"Sit down, Mr. Bardon. I know this is annoying, but think, now, would you be scarcely less annoyed if I were not here?"

"My considered opinion is that I would," Ned Bardon said. "Speak your piece and get out. I'd like to get to bed."

Gray, elfin eyebrows peaked above widening eyes in the fleshy face. "To bed? Ah, but not to sleep. After all, my dear young fellow, you've just killed a man."

Ned Bardon sank slowly into a chair. The muscles around his mouth were tight. Schoenling briskly hitched a chair near his unwilling host and squatted on the edge of it. Schoenling's smile showed yellow, pointed teeth.

"Killed a man," he repeated, nodding. "Gets you, doesn't it? I use the word 'man' loosely, of course. Jake Katz, alias Robert Harbin, alias a few other names, was a gunman, bank robber, drug addict, lady chaser, and, inasmuch as I am a broad-minded individual, I'd say you've done your good turn for the day. But the police, now—" the big face sobered—"they're rather narrow in their interpretations. Murder in any one of several degrees is nonetheless murder, even if the exterminated one happens to be a human rat."

Ned Bardon's hands clenched on the arms of the chair. "Murder, hell! I hung one on him and he cracked his head open on a fireplug when he fell. There was a girl—" He broke off and hope welled up within him. The fat man was nodding as though he had witnessed the whole thing.

"I was there," he said, "in one of those parked cars. I saw the whole thing."

"Then—" Ned Bardon's smile was tentative—"you'll explain to the police?"

Schoenling removed the cigar stump from his mouth. His lips pursed and his elfin brows gathered in a frown of dismay. "The police? Dear me, I hope it doesn't come to that. It needn't. It's entirely up to you, of course, but if I *do* have to tell the police, I shall tell them that you and Jake Katz were quarreling over that entrancing bit of fluff.

"I shall tell them that the girl went out with poor Jake, and that you waylaid him and killed him in a jealous frenzy. You see, my dear fellow? You grasp the unenviable position I can put you in, if I so desire?"

Ned Bardon's mouth fell loosely open. He closed it over a short profane word. "Who in the hell do you think you could get to believe you?"

"Any number of people," Schoenling said pleasantly. "Believe me, my dear boy, I am an accomplished liar."

"I never saw the girl in my life. I didn't even see her tonight, for that matter. I wouldn't know her if she walked in the door right now."

"Perhaps. Perhaps not," the fleshy man admitted. "But you miss the point. I—" he thumbed his chest—"*I* know the young woman in question. Further, I know exactly where she may be found, and I am reasonably certain she can be persuaded to sign an affidavit to the effect that you were jealous of Jake Katz. And that she saw you kill him. And that, I think, would be quite enough to send you to the electric chair."

NED BARDON stood up. His fists clenched, his arms hanging loosely at his sides as the fat man gestured slightly with the left hand that remained in the pocket of the loose-knit white linen coat.

"How much, you damned blackmailer?"

"Oh, tut! Let me remind you, Mr. Bardon, that it was you, not I, who originally mentioned the possibility of my going to the police. I was merely pointing out how prettily you'd frame. Actually, I've done you a great favor—a favor which I can undo with considerably less trouble than the doing required.

"I've cleaned up the mess for you. Temporarily, at least. If you agree to fulfill certain requirements which I shall eventually make, I see no reason why anyone need ever know exactly what became of Jake Katz."

Ned Bardon's eyes narrowed. "That I don't get."

The fat man waved huge hands. "The body. The bloody mess you left on the sidewalk. It isn't there now, thanks to me." He smiled broadly. "Won't you rest better, knowing that? Aren't you the least bit grateful to Fat Paul?"

Ned Bardon didn't say anything. That tight, trapped feeling hadn't lessened.

Schoenling said, "Shall I go on?"

"I can't stop you."

Schoenling laughed. "No, you can't. Yet there's nothing of

the sadist about me. I shan't turn the screw unless you make me. Rather, I should like to extend the hand of partnership."

"That's damned generous of you," Ned Bardon said with a short laugh.

"It is indeed. I have in my possession certain securities, negotiable, which I may have a little trouble disposing of—except at an outrageous discount."

"You mean they're stolen," Ned Bardon said flatly.

The fat man laughed. "Quite. You're an alert young man. You are indeed. Further, you are the trusted employee of the firm of Earhart and Cline, Investment Brokers. With the prestige of that organization behind you, I have not the slightest doubt that you can dispose of these securities to our mutual advantage. No, don't shake your head like that."

"You go to hell," Ned Bardon said.

"Oh, cheerfully." Schoenling stood, both hands in his jacket pockets, a benign smile on his big face. "I'll go to hell sometime after I have gone to the police. Sometime, I might add, after you've gone to the chair."

Ned Bardon swayed slightly forward. For a brief instant he closed his eyes and saw his future tumbling about him, crushing him in the refuse. All of his carefully laid plans could be smashed by a word from the fat man who faced him across the room. He'd lose everything. He'd lose Ann, and she was everything.

"Wait," he said huskily.

"Gladly," Schoenling said. He moved to the door. "Fat Paul, you will find, is the most patient of men. I shall wait until tomorrow." He corked his small mouth with the cold stump of his cigar and opened the door. "Good night to you," he said pleasantly and stepped into the hall.

Ned Bardon watched the door close. He listened to the receding footsteps. Except for the sweat that plastered his shirt across his chest, there was no outward indication of emotion. It was all choked up inside, deep in his guts—an inner trembling that he couldn't get hold of.

He moved, finally, with wooden strides, into the kitchenette where he got a glass and poured generously from a bottle of rye whiskey to which he added a little water. Maybe this would do it—ease his high-strung nerves. If he could relax he'd be able to think. There must be a way out of a mess like this. There damned well *had* to be.

HE TASTED his drink, turned back to the connecting door where he stood for a moment, the glass in his hand, his head cocked as he listened to a faint electric hum that came from within the living room itself. And then his startled gaze sprang to the radio record player on the little cabinet ten feet from where he stood.

The turntable and its white disk were spinning. The pick-up arm moved to the edge of the record, lowered. An oath broke from Ned Bardon's lips as he strode toward the record player. And then he paused, his extended hand arrested inches above the pick-up arm on the machine as a soft feminine voice spoke from the loudspeaker grill of the radio console.

"Hello, darling, wherever you are. I have so much to say to you and this disk is so small. Yet if it was as large as the earth itself and played until the end of time it could not hold all the love I have for you. You see, my dear—"

Ned Bardon lifted the pick-up arm, cut the player switch with an angry gesture.

"Say, I'm sorry about that."

"Wh-what?" Ned Bardon stammered. He turned stiffly. There had been another voice, a man's, and it had come from behind him. Yet there was no one there. No one in the room at all except Ned Bardon. The inner trembling broke through the taut surface of his body. His hand shook, his drink slopped.

"I must be out of my mind," he murmured.

There was a sigh. *"I get everlastingly tired of people thinking they're going crazy,"* the voice said, *"and looking pop-eyed whenever I make my presence known. Sit down, Bardon, you're spilling your drink. It's Captain Zero."*

Bardon continued to stare at empty air. He had heard of Captain Zero, a man who, according to newspaper accounts, had somehow mastered the art of invisibility and whose untiring efforts against crime and political corruption had become front page copy from coast to coast.

It was, Bardon had believed, a good story, something you could kick around and talk about. It was no more fantastic than flying disks and neither was it—to Ned Bardon's way of thinking—any less fantastic. But to hear a matter-of-fact, a not unpleasant, an even earthy voice coming out of nowhere to announce that it was Captain Zero, was something else.

He'd read about such things, he'd laughed, and now it was actually happening to him. Captain Zero was in Ned Bardon's own living room. Captain Zero was more than a voice—he was a person of some substance. Ned Bardon felt a gentle pressure against his chest as though a hand were urging him to back up to the nearest chair. He sat down.

The voice was saying, *"I thought just this once I'd make my presence known with a musical fanfare or something of the sort. That's why I turned on your record player. I really had no intention of prying into your love-life, Bardon."*

Ned Bardon said tonelessly, "It doesn't matter." He lifted his glass and drank deeply before it occurred to him that that probably wasn't very polite in the presence of his distinguished guest. "Whiskey?" he invited. "Will you help yourself?"

"No thanks. I'm not at all sure it wouldn't show."

"Show?" Ned Bardon blinked. And then he started to laugh. "Like a thermometer, I suppose."

Zero was moving about the room and Bardon was fully aware of it. He could hear the faint stir of sound. He could see the nap of the rug depressed by invisible feet—tracks that moved from chair to chair. Finally the chair with its cotton tapestry upholstery moved as though of its own accord across the room until it faced Ned Bardon. He saw the cushions of back and bottom cave under the weight of his unseen guest. Captain Zero had sat down.

"How the devil did you get in?" Bardon asked curiously. "You don't ooze through keyholes, do you?"

"I came in with Schoenling," Zero replied. *"Kept off the rug, of course. Kept my mouth shut, too."*

"And your ears open?" Ned Bardon persisted uneasily.

"That's right. Now listen, Bardon, I need your help. I've got to cover a lot of ground in a hurry."

Ned Bardon's laugh broke in. "I'm in a dandy spot to help anybody. You heard Schoenling, didn't you? I killed a guy tonight."

"So I gathered. Care to give me the details?"

NED BARDON nodded. "I'd dropped in at Melton's Bowling Alley shortly before midnight. I happened to be in the neighborhood and I thought I'd look up an old friend, name of Scott Murphy. He and I used to hang around there a lot. But I'd missed Murph. I left the alley at a minute or so past midnight, and was headed for my car when this girl came running to me. Some guy was chasing her. You know Jessop Street?"

"Yes."

"Well, it was as black as the inside of your hat." Ned Bardon laughed. "Maybe not *your* hat, but you get the idea. This girl asked me to help her. She practically forced me to, as a matter of fact. The man hit me, I let him have one, and he went down and cracked his head on a fireplug. That killed him, apparently.

"When I looked around, the girl was a block up the street, running like hell. There I was, stuck with the corpse, scared half out of my wits. I took off—a dumb thing to do—and that, with whatever trimmings Schoenling can provide, can finish me in the worst way."

Ned Bardon lifted his glass, drained it, put it down on the arm of his chair. He stared at the spot where Zero sat, eyes narrow and glinting, a slight smile on his lips.

"Unless," Ned Bardon said, "you feel like going to bat for me,

Captain. You heard Schoenling, didn't you? You know it's to be a frame, and you can testify—"

"I'm afraid it's not that easy," the voice of Zero interrupted. *"Maybe you've never thought a whole lot about what it's like to be invisible. You can't possibly conceive of its disadvantages. As an investigator, I can't pick up a material clue, for example, without giving myself away. I can't conceal anything on my person. I have a lot of trouble with doors.*

"When I tackle a crime, about all I can do is get information to the police or else catch the criminal red-handed and hold him until the police get there. Everything has to be self-evident and conclusive for the simple reason that I can't take the witness stand in court. For that reason, I can't testify in your behalf."

Ned Bardon's face contorted. "Then I'm sunk." He ran a hand distractedly through his blond hair. "You heard what Schoenling wants me to do—peddle hot securities for him. It's that or the chair."

"And you haven't the slightest idea who the girl was that you rescued tonight?"

Ned Bardon shook his head. "She was any girl. Then again, she may have had two heads—I wouldn't know."

"You think it might have been a put-up job?"

THE YOUNG man considered that for a moment. "No. This Jake Katz hit his head on the fire hydrant. You can't make anything more out of that. It's just a run of bad luck, and Schoenling decided to capitalize on it."

Zero's voice broke an interval of thoughtful silence. *"Maybe I can get at the girl."*

"How can you when we don't know who she is?"

"Maybe I can find out. If I can, if I can get to her, I may be able to break the frame. In the meantime, you can help me by pretending to fall in with Schoenling. If you can't get in on the inside of this thing—"

"What thing?" Ned Bardon interrupted sharply.

"I'm not sure. I thought at first it was just a series of well-planned safe and vault robberies. That's why I have been tailing Schoenling. He's a fence. He might be the brains behind the mob, I don't know. But there's more to it than breaks into print. Two of the heaviest losers to this mob of gunmen have been murdered—Tom McAlister and George Moffet."

"You're sure about that, Captain? I'd heard there was some talk that McAlister didn't kill himself, but I thought old George Moffet died of heart failure. They were both clients of mine."

"Moffet died of heart failure, all right," Zero admitted. *"He was on a diet that included thyroid extract tablets. Somebody substituted some of his thyroid pills for a simple digestive remedy which he habitually took in large quantities. The result was that he got an overdose of thyroid which brought on the heart attack that killed him.*

"It was subtle, carefully planned murder. Like McAlister, Moffet was completely alone in the world. In fact, they both belonged to that well-known Bachelors' Club here in Pendleville. Tonight, a third member of that club was killed."

Ned Bardon's face was blank. "I don't get it."

"Neither do I."

"Who was it? I guess I've sold securities to most of those old-timers in that crowd."

"Duncan Moore."

"You're kidding."

"I'm afraid not."

"But good lord—" Ned Bardon broke off and looked at the watch on his wrist. "Look, Captain, I was over there until nearly midnight. Until eleven-thirty, anyway. Moore lives right across the alley on Broadmoor Avenue. He had me come over to talk about some securities he intended to sell. He was perfectly all right. His usual crabbed self. The houseboy was there—"

"I haven't got the details yet," Zero interrupted, and his voice came from near the open window overlooking Piedmont Street rather than the chair opposite Ned Bardon. *"But I imagine we'll both hear about it any time now. A police car just stopped out in front."*

Ned Bardon stood up. Cold sweat trickled from beneath his armpits. "What the hell am I going to do?"

"Do?" Zero's voice was soft. *"Tell a straight story. About your visit to Duncan Moore's apartment this evening, that is. The other matter—about Jake Katz in Jessop Street—isn't likely to come up if Schoenling is shooting straight with you. But I've got to know your decision. Are you going to help me get at the Schoenling crowd from the inside?"*

Ned Bardon chewed his lip. "I don't know."

"You'd better decide," Zero said somewhat curtly. *"The police are on their way up."*

Ned Bardon stared at the open window. "I've never made a bargain with anybody that I didn't know. If you were something besides a voice and a dent in a chair—if I could see you—"

"You can't and you won't. Come on, Bardon—are you with me, or are you going to try to get out of this mess alone?"

Ned Bardon took a deep breath like a swimmer about to plunge into icy water. He smiled slowly. "With you, Captain."

"Good boy." It was scarcely more than a whisper. *"Then I think we can do it."*

There was a knock at Ned Bardon's door.

CHAPTER 3
THE GLASS KEY

T HE POLICE radio put out the coded dispatch at 12:08 A.M. and Pendleville's chief of police, Ed Cavanaugh, heard it as soon as anybody. At the time, he was rolling along Outer Drive, overlooking the city, at about twenty miles an hour. The dispatch constituted a rude intrusion on a very personal matter.

Ed Cavanaugh said, "Damn."

The very personal matter raised her head from his shoulder and asked, "What's code sixteen, Ed?"

"Homicide."

Miss Doro Kelly, reporter for the Pendleville *World,* straightened and tipped forward on the cushions, thus freeing Ed Cavanaugh's right arm for the unromantic business of steering the police car.

"How perfectly convenient for me," she said.

"That damned thing," Ed Cavanaugh jerked his head to indicate the FM radio. "The next time I talk you into going for a drive with me, I'll roll up to your door in one of the city's ash trucks."

"I'm not sure I'd consent," she said.

"I'm not either." Cavanaugh's growl was lost in the increasing thrum of the engine as the car picked up speed. He had never at any time been sure of anything that Doro Kelly would do or say. "Look, Kelly, there's no time like the present—aren't we going like a bat out of hell to a homicide case? Will you marry me?"

A truck loomed ahead of the speeding police car, and Cavanaugh gave it a blast from his siren. When he had swung around the truck and into the clear, he risked a sidelong glance at the pert profile of the girl beside him.

"I didn't get that," he said.

"Maybe you don't want to get it," she said. "It was a small but quite decided 'No.' Please, Ed—" she put a hand impulsively on his arm—"don't look that way."

"What way?" he snapped.

"Like the last of the cigar store Indians being dragged off to a bonfire."

He said after a moment, "I'll keep on asking, Doro. Every once in a while."

"You do that," she said softly. "A girl has been known to change her mind."

Which left him not without hope. He was in reasonably good spirits when he pulled up in front of the Hildebrand Apartments on Broadmoor Avenue.

"Just seventeen and a half minutes from Outer Drive," he commented after a glance at his watch.

They got out. Cavanaugh strode ahead of the girl to the illuminated entryway. There was a small crowd around the door—curious neighbors asking questions of Patrolman Davis.

"The Press?" Cavanaugh asked Davis in passing.

"They're holding them upstairs, Chief."

"Right." Cavanaugh waited for Doro Kelly, touched her arm, and steered her into the elevator. "No special privileges. And none of that stuff about being a distant relative of the corpse."

Doro Kelly rolled lovely blue eyes up at him. "But how do I know, Chief? Some of the Kelly family must have had a strain of lace-curtain Irish in them somewhere."

And then they were getting out at the fourth floor corridor which was short and wide, with two doors on opposite sides. The door on the right, Cavanaugh observed, carried a small brass plate with the word *Deliveries* embossed upon it.

The other door was open, bottle-necked by a couple of uniformed police who were holding off the gentlemen of the press and certain other individuals who belonged in neighboring apartments on lower floors. Cavanaugh also noticed that Doro Kelly looked eagerly among the other reporters, possibly in hope of spotting her colleague, Lee Allyn.

Well, Cavanaugh thought, she would not find Mr. Allyn. While Cavanaugh had no notion as to the present whereabouts of that young man, he was nevertheless confident that Doro Kelly would not be seeing her fellow reporter at this hour of the night. Nor would anyone else.

Lee Allyn was Captain Zero. Cavanaugh, and Cavanaugh alone, knew that.

HE LEFT Doro Kelly in the hall, entered the vestibule and then the spacious living room. There a plump woman of about fifty, with prominent eyes beneath pinkish curling bangs, was talking to an elderly bald man with spritely ears. A young Filipino wearing something that closely approached a zoot suit lounged with one leg thrown over the arm of his chair, chewed gum, and was answering the questions put to him by Detective Norb Riley.

Cavanaugh would have gone directly to the door of an adjoining room where Lieutenant Beckridge of Homicide was standing, had not the woman with the pink bangs discovered the presence of the police chief. She deserted the old man with the pointed ears and scuttled to Cavanaugh.

"What are we to do, Chief Cavanaugh?" she demanded. "A thoroughly respectable neighborhood such as this—it's horrible! How do I know I won't be murdered in my bed some night?"

It was, Cavanaugh explained patiently, an exceedingly remote possibility. The law of averages was against it. Though, of course, every precaution would be taken.

He escaped to Beckridge, a man older than Cavanaugh, whose gray eyes had a worried gleam.

"Number three," Beckridge said. "McAlister, Moffet, and now Duncan Moore. Walter Bedlaws, the bald man over there—he's one of them. All members of the same club, and what the hell is this, Chief?"

Cavanaugh shook his head. He didn't know. Open season on wealthy old bachelors, it looked like.

He said, "Let's get at it."

Beckridge opened the door. Flush with the frame on either side were bookshelves extending from floor to ceiling. Beckridge kicked aside a rubber-covered electrical cord and plug, and led Cavanaugh into a room that was nearly square, comfortably furnished, and snug.

Damned snug, Cavanaugh reflected, for a hot night like this. The wall that fronted on the street had steel casements which

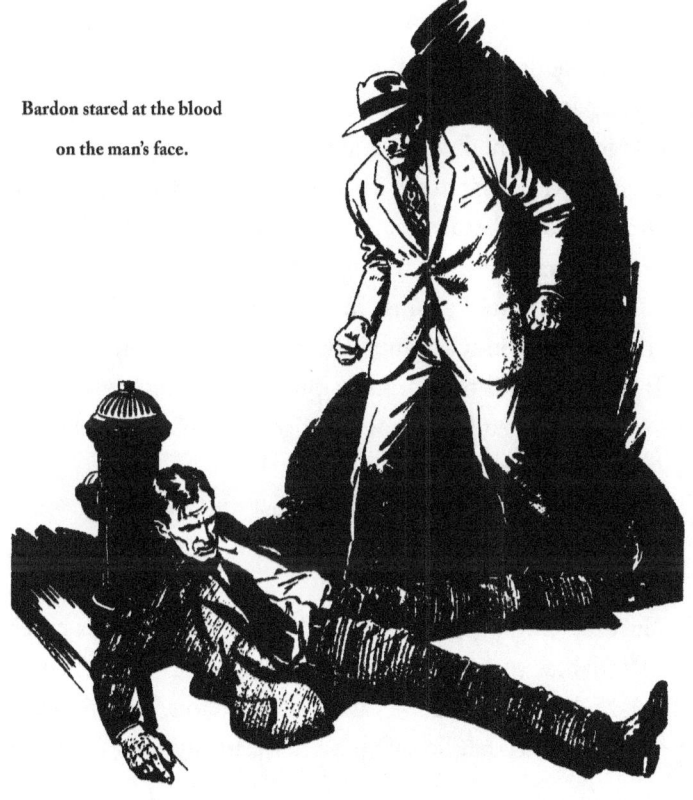

Bardon stared at the blood
on the man's face.

were opened and tightly screened. Another wall was covered with maps. One good oil painting on the wall opposite the bookshelves and a door which, Cavanaugh observed, led into the master bedroom.

There was a walnut desk in the center of the floor. It held a typewriter, three scrapbooks, and an ice bucket with an open bottle of champagne in it. There were two half-filled glasses of what was presumably champagne sitting on the green blotter. The furniture included a red leather lounge chair, a mantel type radio on one of the book shelves to the right of the door, and Duncan Moore's wheelchair close to the windows, flanked by a small table piled high with scrapbooks and newspapers.

Duncan Moore sat in the wheelchair which had not been visible from the door because of the flanking bookshelves. He faced the bedroom, his wasted figure slumped, silvery head forward until his chin rested against his sunken chest. He looked, in death, like somebody's grandfather dozing in the sun.

It was not until the coroner's physician straightened away from the body that Cavanaugh noticed the small round bullet hole in the center of the old man's forehead.

"That did it?" Cavanaugh asked. "Just the one?"

"That's about enough," the doctor said, "if it happens to be in the right place."

"Just so." Cavanaugh turned to Beckridge. "Who was here?"

"We'd like to know. The houseboy had gone out to an all-night drugstore to get a carton of cigarettes. The entrances were locked, but that doesn't have to mean anything because a couple of Moore's friends have keys, and the houseboy says he lost his on the way to the drugstore.

"Which," Beckridge added, "doesn't have to mean anything either. Manuel might've swallowed his own key in an effort to place himself beyond suspicion. Locked himself out, see, and therefore couldn't have got in to plug the old man."

Cavanaugh said that he saw. "Who have we got beside Manuel?"

"Walter Bedlows, who lives about eight blocks from here. We brought him over here because Bedlows was Moore's closest friend. Bedlows admits he has a key."

"Who's the woman with the pink bangs?"

"A Miss Franzer, a buyer for Yoder's Department Store. She lives on the floor below. She heard the shots and 'phoned head-quarters, which places the time at two minutes after midnight."

"Shots, you said."

BECKRIDGE NODDED. "What Miss Franzer insists was a 'volley.' I'll show you." Beckridge waited until the doctor stepped out of the way and then stepped in close to the wheel-chair in which the dead man sat. He pointed to the floor that stretched between the wheelchair and the windows.

There was a circular nickel-plated object with a trigger-like lever on the side. It looked like one of those automatic fly reels for fishermen. Cavanaugh got down on one knee for a closer inspection.

"Oh, sure," he said, remembering. "One of those."

It was a blank cartridge shooting device which had been marketed some years ago. When loaded and wound, it would fire six .22 caliber blank cartridges in rapid succession at the touch of a trigger. This was supposed to scare off an intruder. Sometimes, Cavanaugh supposed, something like that might work. Tonight it hadn't. He stood and turned to the medical man.

"If you're through, I am. How about you, Beck?"

Beckridge said, "Through. We got pix."

"You'd better try that scare gun for prints," Cavanaugh suggested. "We'll take the houseboy first. No, the woman— what's her name? In here, just as soon as they take away the body."

Cavanaugh moved over to the desk. He stooped, sniffed at the champagne in the glasses. It smelled like champagne. It looked like flat champagne. He sat gingerly on the edge of the desk, crossed his ankles, folded his arms. His dark face was stoical as his eyes ranged around the room.

You could, Cavanaugh thought, sum up Duncan Moore as one of life's spectators. Certainly, since arthritis had taken a firm hold of him, he had not been a participant in at least a decade. But then he hadn't allowed himself to go to seed. His books, his maps, his radio, his clippings—he'd known what was going on in the world. An interested observer of the passing show, grow-ing wise and mellow with the years, harming no one. Just a nice old man. And then death walked in.

Cavanaugh's fingers gripped the edge of the desk and discov-ered a sticky lump beneath the ledge. He moved his hand, lifted it, and smelled at the fingertips. His mouth quirked distastefully.

"Somebody's gum."

"Yeah." Lieutenant Beckridge moved away from the door

to allow the tour men from the morgue to come in. "All over the place. Some people have a special spot like the piano, but Manuel parks his anywhere he happens to be. There's even some on the doorstop. I got into it when I plugged in the floodlights for Koontz."

The doorstop Beckridge was talking about was brass with a rubber tip, and it had been screwed into the bottom rail of the door connecting the library with the living room.

"What about that doorstop?" Cavanaugh asked. And then, as the tour men swung the door wide to get out with their unpleasant burden, Cavanaugh understood the unusual placement of the doorstop. Had the bumper been attached to the base molding of the bookcases it would have made a dandy thing to trip over.

And that was the way with material clues at the scene of a crime: something stuck out like a sore thumb and there was usually a very innocent reason for its being where it was. Cavanaugh expected more of people than he did of things, but after half an hour of questioning these, he realized that he and Beckridge had very little.

First there was this Miss Ada Franzer who had been on the point of retiring for the night when she had heard the "volley" of gunfire in the apartment above. She had felt it her civic duty to call the police and seemed rather disappointed that Cavanaugh didn't immediately hang a medal on her.

Murder, she said, was not nearly as revolting as she had imagined. Stimulating and exciting, she found it, though it certainly did have a way of upsetting one's schedule.

So much for Miss Franzer. There was one at every killing, and it was nice that this one was so absolutely certain about the time of the shots.

WALTER BEDLOWS was next, and when he was ushered into the library and saw the empty wheelchair, his pendulous lower lip trembled and he sniffled a little. He had spent many a peaceful evening in this room with Duncan Moore. They'd played chess sometimes. Sometimes they had talked of current topics. But more often they had been content to enjoy each other's company in virtual silence.

But not this evening. As a matter of fact, he hadn't been in Duncan Moore's apartment for the past month. There'd been some slight difference of opinion—hardly a quarrel—over the State Department's position on China.

"Were these evenings together usually brightened by a bottle of champagne?" Cavanaugh persisted.

"Well—" Bedlows' eyes shifted to the glasses on the desk— "sherry usually. One New Year's Eve it was champagne, but it was usually sherry."

"Did Duncan Moore have any enemies?" Cavanaugh asked.

Bedlows shook his bald head vigorously. "None beyond our mutual enemy."

Cavanaugh frowned. "I don't get it."

"Death." Bedlows said huskily. "We're all members—were, that is—of the Bachelors' Club. We're old men, waiting. Lonely old fools who have made a sort of game of our survival. You have heard of Tontine insurance, haven't you?"

Beckridge and Cavanaugh exchanged glances. Cavanaugh's

gaze returned to the bland round face of Walter Bedlows. "You mean one of those last-man things? The last one of you alive gets the face value of the policy?"

"Something like that." Bedlows hooked his thumbs in the belt loops of his brown pants and drummed silently on his melon of a paunch. "If you ask me, there is one among us who is determined to be the last man, in order to claim the tidy sum of five hundred thousand dollars for himself. McAlister is gone. Then George Moffet. Now poor old Duncan. That's three out of the eight. One among us is a murderer. It is not, believe me, at all pleasant to be one of the remaining five. And it is terrible to cast an eye about the circle of your closest friends and think, 'One of you intends to kill me.'"

Walter Bellows waved a hand toward the desk. "There's your proof. Champagne for a friend. One of Duncan Moore's friends sat here, drank with him, and then shot him."

Cavanaugh grunted. "Just a second, Mr. Bedlows." He turned to Beckridge. "See if they've lifted anything off that scare gun and bring it in here."

Beckridge stepped out into the living room, returned a moment later with the cartridge shooting device which he handed to Cavanaugh.

"No prints except those of the victim," the lieutenant said.

Cavanaugh held the device in his palm. "Ever see this, Mr. Bedlows?"

The bald man nodded. "He got it some years ago when there was an epidemic of burglaries in town. It shoots blanks."

"Exactly," Cavanaugh said. "Not the sort of thing you'd have on hand if you expected to entertain a friend." He smiled slightly. "That's all for now, Mr. Bedlows. And thanks."

The bald man rose. He said stiffly, "Nevertheless, my opinion remains unaltered. You will find the murderer among the five remaining members of our Bachelors' Club. The last one alive is your killer. Wait and see."

Cavanaugh didn't think that "wait and see" represented a very practical attitude. He turned to Beckridge with a sigh.

"Let's have the houseboy now. Getting any ideas, Beck?"

"Not a one. Except that regardless of how nutty it sounds, I think we ought to look into what Bedlows says about this Bachelors' Club. Five hundred grand ain't hay."

MANUEL, THE dead man's servant, was twenty-five, small, his dark face prematurely withered, his eyes sharp and black. He slumped in the red leather chair, one leg over an arm of it, chewed his gum, and stared insolently at the two police.

He said, "I don't know from nothing. I wasn't here. The old duck was alive and kicking when I left and when I got back from the drugstore you cops were here. Maybe you killed him."

Cavanaugh stared at Manuel in silence until the black eyes shifted uneasily. Then Cavanaugh indicated the champagne on the desk.

"Before you left for the drugstore, Mr. Moore had you bring this bottle of champagne, didn't he?"

"He did not. Mr. Bardon brought that with him when he came to see the old duck tonight. I iced it, brought it in here along with the glasses. The old man told me he wouldn't need me unless he rang. And he rang at 11:40 when Mr. Bardon was ready to go."

"This Bardon—" Cavanaugh began.

"He lives over on Piedmont," Manuel supplied. "Ned Bardon. He works for an investment broker."

"Ned Bardon," Cavanaugh repeated. He looked over at Beckridge who nodded, moved to the door of the library, and went out.

"All right now, Manuel," Cavanaugh said. "Let's go back over this pretty carefully. When you were opening the champagne in here did you catch any of the conversation that passed between Bardon and your employer?"

Manuel shook his head. "Mainly because I didn't open the champagne. I told you I put the bottle in the ice bucket, brought it in here with the two glasses, and left the two alone. At 11:40 the old man buzzed me. I came from my room, and Bardon was standing in the door here, ready to leave. Old Moore was in the wheelchair."

"What did they say?"

"What a nice evening it was," Manuel replied. "Stuff like that. They both said goodnight, Bardon closed the door, and I showed him to the front door and went out with him."

"Why did you do that?" Cavanaugh persisted. "Was there any reason for it?"

"He wanted to show me his new car. He's got a Caddy half a block long. He gave me a lift to the drugstore and I walked back."

"If you lost your key, how did you expect to get back in?" Cavanaugh asked.

Manuel shrugged. "Old Moore would've let me in. He can get around some, in and out of his chair. He'd have let me in."

Then, Cavanaugh thought, Duncan Moore could also have got out of the wheelchair to get the scare gun. It wasn't as though he'd been waiting there all evening, expecting trouble, with the device clutched in his hand. It didn't have to be that way at all, though it might have been.

Walter Bedlows' theory that the killer was a friend could be right. Moore and the unknown might have quarreled here tonight. Moore might have tried to force the other to leave, might have got and used the shooting device as an audible threat. Then the other might have pulled a real gun, believing that he or she were acting in self defense.

Cavanaugh picked up the shooting device and showed it to Manuel who admitted having seen it around.

"In the bedroom on the nightstand mostly. The old man was scared of burglars and twice as scared of firearms."

Cavanaugh settled back on the edge of the desk. "Now to get back to this Bardon. Was he a fairly regular visitor?"

"Sometimes twice a month, but not regular. A couple of times since I've been working here, I had to wheel the old man over to see Bardon. That's about the only place he went except to the Bachelors' Club. And then—" the small brown face crinkled with laughter—"then damned if he wouldn't get all dolled up and take a taxi with nothing to assist him except his cane. Didn't want the rest of the old coots to know how bad off he was, I figure. They've got some kind of a bet up as to who'll live the longest. Some sort of jackpot."

MANUEL BROKE off as the door of the library was opened by Beckridge. From across the living room beyond came the sound of laughter. Cavanaugh, who had never been able to see anything funny about a murder investigation, stepped to the door.

"Can't they keep those reporters quiet out there, Beck?" he asked testily.

Beckridge said, "I'll see what I can do about that. Riley is here with Bardon."

Cavanaugh grunted. He was already appraising Ned Bardon from a distance. The slight, tall man with Riley had unruly blond hair and fair skin. He was not outstandingly handsome— clean-looking, rather, with stubborn chin and clear, intelligent appearing eyes. There was a resiliency about him. None of that pseudo-toughness that a jerk like Manuel flaunted. It was something deeper than that.

Cavanaugh's attention was again drawn toward the entryway where the reporters were gathered.

"Try the gadget on him, Pagget," somebody said.

There was prolonged laughter.

"Sure, Pagget, maybe Cavanaugh'll let you bloodhound for him with that thing."

Cavanaugh swore softly, strode past Beckridge and across the living room. The two police who guarded the entrance sobered immediately as the police chief approached. The reporters were gathered about a gangling, untidy man with fuzzy gray hair who wore an earphone that was kept in place by a piece of black spring steel across his flat head.

He was carrying a small black box that looked as though it might have been a homemade portable radio. Whatever it was that he heard from the earphone, had transported him beyond the reach of the reporter's jeers. His wide brown eyes held an expression of ecstasy.

"Now what?" Cavanaugh demanded harshly.

Somebody gave the man with the box a push that wedged him between the two cops. Doro Kelly's clear, lilting voice called:

"See if Cavanaugh radiates anything, Pagget."

The man ripped the headphone off and thrust it toward Cavanaugh. "Listen, Chief," he said excitedly.

Cavanaugh made no move to take the earphone. "Who in the hell are you?"

"Wayland Pagget." The untidy man fumbled the 'phone up to his own ear and fiddled with knobs on the black box.

Cavanaugh remembered where he had seen the man's face before. Wayland Pagget was science editor of the *World* and his picture appeared above his weekly column. What he was doing at the scene of a murder investigation Cavanaugh didn't know. He put out a hand and pulled the earpiece away from Pagget's head.

"What are you doing here?"

Soft brown eyes looked as though they were not entirely sure. "Why, I live here," Pagget recalled. "First floor. I just completed this Geiger counter and I wanted to find somebody with a luminous watch so I could check the counter for sensitivity. There was a crowd in front of the apartment, and I thought sure somebody would have a luminous watch."

"I haven't," Cavanaugh snapped.

"And then your man Riley and that other chap came along," Pagget continued, "and the Geiger counter started to tick furiously. Listen for yourself. I simply followed Riley and the other chap up here. I could have done it blind."

Cavanaugh looked back over his shoulder to where Riley and Ned Bardon were standing. Riley coughed embarrassedly.

"It's not me. Chief. I haven't got a luminous watch. If you ask me, the guy is nuts."

"But there are definite and strong emanations," Pagget insisted. There was loud laughter from the press.

"Maybe Riley has a pocketful of uranium."

"Yeah, maybe that's what it takes to bribe a good cop in this atomic age."

Which was considerably more than enough for Cavanaugh. He pushed Pagget back through the door.

"And listen, you guys," he said, "and gals—there'll be no hand-out until we're damned good and ready. You might just as well go get some sleep. Try me downtown, sometime after daylight."

CAVANAUGH SLAMMED the door on grumbling protests, turned, strode back to the library. Manuel was standing in the library door, a grin on his brown face, and as Cavanaugh looked past the servant into the empty room he saw something that brought him to an abrupt halt.

One of the champagne glasses was elevated a good eighteen inches from the surface of the desk. It remained suspended in thin air for an instant, tilted as though to invisible lips. And then the glass descended quickly and surely, its base making a faint click against the desk top.

Cavanaugh's indrawn breath was audible but his face remained the same wooden Indian mask. Captain Zero was in the room. Either he had been there all along or he had slipped in with Riley and Ned Bardon. Well, that was all right with Cavanaugh. Before this thing was finished, he had a notion, he'd welcome any sort of assistance that the phenomenal Zero had to offer.

Cavanaugh turned to the houseboy. "Okay for now," he said. And to Beckridge, "Let's have Mr. Bardon."

The blond young man in the living room heard what Cavanaugh had said. Instead of waiting for Riley to steer him to the library, Ned Bardon stepped forward eagerly. As he passed the departing Manuel, his loosely closed left hand brushed the side of the houseboy's jacket.

It was smoothly, casually done, almost too bald a move to suggest deception; yet deception it was, and Cavanaugh was instantly aware of it. He lunged and caught the startled houseboy by the tail of his over-long coat, and at the same time Cavanaugh managed to nip Ned Bardon's left sleeve.

"That was good," Cavanaugh commented dryly, "but not good enough—that lateral pass or whatever it was."

Ned Bardon's face was waxy, his blue eyes shiny with alarm as he watched Cavanaugh spin Manuel around and dip into the side pocket of the houseboy's coat. There were cigarettes, a lighter, a package of gum, and a key, the metal surface of which was still warm and moist from Ned Bardon's sweating palm.

Cavanaugh held the key in his hand, tossed and caught it, his gaze shifting from Manuel to Bardon. The latter moistened dry lips. His smile was tentative and flickering.

"I can explain that," he began.

"Is this the key you lost, Manuel?" Cavanaugh wanted to know.

"Sure, but—"

"I found it on the cushions of my car after I gave Manuel a lift down to the drugstore earlier this evening." Bardon was saying. He shifted his feet uneasily. His blue eyes moved to Lieutenant Beckridge where they found no sympathy at all.

"Honestly," Ned Bardon said, "the thing never entered my mind until right now. Then I got to thinking, 'Suppose they search me.' Don't you see? It wouldn't look good, would it? I had that key in my possession? Under the circumstances," he concluded lamely.

"Not," Cavanaugh said, "under the circumstances. I'll buy that, Bardon. That part about it not looking good, I'll buy."

CHAPTER 4
A WEAPON OF THE DEVIL!

IN THE bedroom of the dingy flat over the Fidelity Pawn Shop, the telephone rang. Paul Schoenling came awake with a grunt and turned over on his white enameled iron bed. It creaked and trembled beneath his weight. The clock on the little Victorian table said 4:30 A.M., not an unusual hour for Schoenling's 'phone to ring. He picked up the handset without lifting his huge head from the pillow.

"Fat Paul?"

"Yes," Schoenling admitted. The voice had an unnatural, muffled sound and he couldn't find a face in his mental rogues' gallery that fitted it.

"I've got something for you."

"You have indeed?" Schoenling raised an elfin eyebrow. "Who's talking?"

"The name wouldn't mean anything. I know Jake Katz. That good enough?"

"Possibly. Possibly not," Schoenling returned cautiously.

"It's good enough," the voice insisted harshly. "I'll be at your back door in five minutes. I'll expect to get in." And the connection was broken.

Schoenling put down the 'phone. He yawned, knuckled his puffy eyelids, then sat up and extended his thick legs over the edge of the bed. Somebody who knew Jake Katz, he mused as he toe-groped for slippers. Somebody—to put it exactly—who *had known* Jake Katz.

That wasn't the best of references, even in the underworld. Perhaps Schoenling's caller would prove to be some out-of-towner who had run into Jake Katz somewhere. Jake Katz had always been able to create the illusion that he was Very Important People.

As he pulled his scarlet, black-piped robe over his huge shoulders, it occurred to Schoenling that he ought to think more kindly of Jake Katz. He had been worth very little to Paul Schoenling while alive, but dead, Jake Katz would prove invaluable.

Jake's sudden and unexpected demise had placed Ned Bardon in Schoenling's grasp. Bardon, if Schoenling was any judge of character, was vigorous and capable. He came equipped with a spotless reputation. He might easily become Schoenling's most useful tool—all through the mere fact that Jake Katz had been born with a skull like an eggshell.

"I ought," Schoenling said aloud, "to erect a tablet in honor of Jake Katz's thin skull." Chuckling, he tied the sash of his robe, turned with an abruptness that belied his weight, and opened the drawer of the table beside the bed. He took out a small flat black automatic pistol which he dropped into the left pocket of his robe.

"Because," he mused aloud, "one never knows, does one?" He left the bedroom to descend a narrow flight of stairs that communicated with his office. The windows of the room were covered with louvred shutters, the door was deadlocked, and there was a burglar alarm system which Schoenling switched off as he heard a knock at the door. His hand dropped into the left hand pocket of his robe, closed comfortably about the little gun.

"Come in, come in," he said brusquely, standing back from the door. As his caller emerged from dark, Schoenling's gray eyebrows went up in surprised peaks. Now, he thought, I've seen everything.

THE MAN who entered the room wore black—hat, raincoat, and cotton gloves. Under the hat was a black sateen hood covering his face and neck. It was tucked well down inside the collar of the raincoat.

"Don't you find it a trifle warm?" Schoenling said. His first impulse was to laugh. As a dealer in stolen goods he had entertained dangerous characters ranging from sneak thieves to top-grade public enemies, and not one of them had ever entered his presence masked.

This person, Schoenling thought, must have gained his knowledge of crime from comic strips. However, the fat man's laugh didn't quite mature. The slots of eyes in the black cloth were not conducive to laughter.

"Close the door, Fat Paul."

Schoenling obeyed in haste. As soon as his back was turned, his visitor stepped in close, reached around Schoenling, and gripped Fat Paul's left wrist. Hand and gun were torn out of the pocket with such violence that the cloth ripped. Schoenling's forehead smacked against the panel of his own door while his left arm strained back and up between his shoulder blades in a hammer-lock.

"Drop it, Fat Paul," said the man in the black hood softly. "Do I make myself clear?"

Schoenling let go of the little gun which slid diagonally across his back and clattered to the floor. The man in black yanked Schoenling around, roughed Schoenling's face with the corded seams of a glove, brought up a knee to Schoenling's paunch in a kick that doubled him over and sent him crabbing backward in the general direction of the desk chair.

Schoenling missed the seat of the chair with his backside,

but a heel caught on a chair leg, and Schoenling went crashing down onto the floor: He sat up, breathing hard, the taste of blood in his mouth. All of his dignity had deserted him. He felt suddenly old and full of physical misery.

Fat Paul came up in a crouch and maneuvered his wide hips onto the edge of the chair.

Paul Schoenling

"Who the devil are you, sir?" he asked with a note of respect.

"I told you I know Jake Katz, and that's enough. I want to talk to you. I'm a stranger in this town, and I've latched onto a sure thing. But I need the men to handle it—men like Jake, handy with a rod. How about it?"

"What's the sure thing?" Schoenling asked.

"A safety deposit box belonging to a man by the name of Duncan Moore. Moore is dead."

Schoenling's eyebrows were quizzically elevated. "You're sure of that?"

"I should be," the man in black said coldly. "I killed him. His safety deposit box will be opened tomorrow for the benefit of the police and tax assessors. It should be a push-over for about six men with plenty of guts."

"You mean loot the box?" Schoenling asked skeptically.

"That's the point," the man in black insisted. "There'll be somebody from headquarters—probably a plainclothesman—a tax official, and the branch bank manager in that booth when the box is open. The tellers will be off guard, what with a cop in the bank. It's a push-over because nobody'll expect anything like that. You've got an outlet for hot bonds, haven't you?" the man in black asked.

"Perhaps," Schoenling said. "Perhaps not. You've cased the bank already, haven't you?"

"I have." The man in black thrust a gloved hand inside his raincoat and brought out a piece of paper on which he had sketched in pencil. "Think you can get the men?" he asked. "You and I aren't in it, of course. We're the brains. Rather, *I'm* the brain and you're in charge of procurement."

"And disposal," Schoenling added, chuckling.

"And disposal," the other repeated. "Now here's the way it stacks up."

DORO KELLY entered the *World* building at 9:30 A.M., and in spite of physical weariness she climbed the short flight of stairs briskly to enter the reception room in front of the editorial offices. There she paused, her head tipped to one side, her eyes on a group of three oak chairs near the receptionist's switchboard. The chairs were remarkable in their emptiness.

Every morning for the past week, when Doro had arrived for work, one of those chairs had been occupied by a cute little thing, all of twenty, with fluffy blond hair and a decided preference for a shade which Doro Kelly had described as "country

54

pink." Figuratively at least, the poor child had clutched in her hot little hand one diploma awarding a B.A. degree. The gold pin on the front of her dress was—in case anybody asked—the crest of an honorary sorority for budding journalists.

The girl had been determined to land a job on the *World*, which was understandable. But what she didn't know—and nobody had seen fit to tell her—was that nothing made red-haired City Editor Fairish gnash his teeth so much as a college graduate who had majored in journalism.

The name the blonde had given was Alice Poynter.

"Where," asked Doro Kelly of Bessy the switchboard operator, "is Sweet Alice, the Daring Girl Reporter?"

Bessy shrugged. "Yesterday afternoon she told me she'd half-sold Fairish on an idea for a feature. Maybe somebody showed her the type lice."

Doro Kelly's sigh was one of mock dismay. "I shall miss the fresh country atmosphere Sweet Alice lent to this sweat-shop." She took long legged strides down the short corridor that was flanked by the offices of various department editors and entered the city room.

Lee Allyn was seated behind his desk, but he'd swiveled his chair around so that his back was toward Fairish, the city editor. Lee's feet were in the lower drawer of the desk, his glasses were pushed up on his forehead almost to the roots of his very blond hair, and his eyes were closed.

Doro Kelly looked at him curiously, a slight smile on her lovely mouth. When he was asleep, as he too frequently was in the *World* office, she thought she saw a certain strength, a fullness of purpose about the cut of Lee Allyn's jaw—attributes which he seemed to close readily when he was awake.

Doro Kelly had often thought, somewhat resignedly, that she'd end up marrying Lee. Or she would go to the opposite extreme and marry the vigorous Ed Cavanaugh. But until she made up her mind between her fellow reporter and the police chief she could dream, couldn't she? She could dream of strong, unseen arms that once had held her. She could dream of that quiet, oddly compelling voice of Captain Zero.

Sometimes in the night she would awake from such a dream. And then, because it was only that, and because of the very hopelessness of loving a person who was wholly invisible, she would sometimes cry a little.

Doro put down her purse and went to the city desk at the rear of the room. Fairish glanced up from his work long enough to push a front page proof of the bulldog edition toward the girl.

"Nice story, Kelly," Fairish commented, which actually amounted to high praise. "See if you can put the benzedrine into Allyn, will you? He's supposed to go over to the city hall and get details on the new traffic ordinance."

Doro said. "He probably won't be interested if it isn't bloodshed."

FAIRISH SNORTED. "If he isn't interested it'll be bloodshed, and guess whose blood. And Kelly—" Fairish leaned wearily back in his chair—"we're going to carry a feature on this Bachelors' Club angle of the McAlister, Moffet, and Moore killings. The five old men who remain playing checkers with death—" Fairish discarded his own figure with a gesture.

"You get the idea. I don't suppose there's anything to it—though that insurance jackpot looks like the best motive turned up so far—but the readers will eat it up. The president of the club will be in sometime this morning, and I'll turn him over to you. Right?"

"Right," Doro agreed. She retraced her steps to stop beside Lee Allyn's chair. "Wake up, boy." She rumpled his thin blond hair playfully. "City Hall. Traffic ordinance, remember? Fairish. Job. Bills. Room rent. Doesn't anything startle you out of that state of suspended animation?"

Lee Allyn took his feet out of the drawer. As he straightened in his chair, his glasses fell automatically into their proper place, his mouth sagged open and he looked—Doro had to admit—a trifle stupid.

She said, smiling, "Dope!"

"My normal reaction when I see anything as breathtakingly lovely as you are," Lee Allyn said.

She was tall and lithe with black hair done in a short, pert bob, with eyes that varied disconcertingly from blue to green. In her simple lime-green dressmaker suit she looked as cool as a julep and twice as intoxicating.

She said, "Fairish is coming to a slow boil."

"There's plenty of time on that traffic ordinance handout," Lee Allyn insisted. "Nobody wants to read about all the new excuses for passing out stickers anyway. What this paper needs is a good crime story."

"Oh?" she said mockingly. "Anything wrong with this?" she

flaunted the front page in his face. "Duncan Moore got it last night, and where were you?"

Lee Allyn took the page of proof from her hands and scanned the streamer with his near-sighted eyes. He whistled softly as though all of this were news to him though actually, as Captain Zero, he had been much closer to what had transpired in the Moore apartment than had Doro Kelly. He had even tasted the flat champagne on the desk of the murder victim.

"Wasn't Moore a member of the Bachelors' Club?" he asked.

She nodded. "Three down and four to go before somebody collects five hundred thousand dollars."

Lee Allyn shook his head. "That's too fantastic. Nobody would shoot at a goal like that. Seven killings out of a possible eight and the guy left alive is guilty? It's nuts!" Allyn's eyes returned to the story as Doro had written it. He read from it aloud:

" 'The champagne, it was revealed, was brought to the apartment by N.A. Bardon employed by a local investment house. Bardon was released by the police after being closely questioned in regard to a key to the Moore apartment found in Bardon's possession. Bardon stated that at the time of the shooting he was in a Jessop Street bowling alley, and this was confirmed by Joseph Melton, proprietor of the alley.' "

Bardon, then, Lee Allyn mused, was momentarily in the clear. There was no mention of Jake Katz's death in the paper, indicating that Schoenling intended to carry out his part of the bargain with Ned Bardon, much to Allyn's satisfaction.

Bardon would be able to assist Captain Zero by boring at

Schoenling's organization from within, and simultaneously Bardon could serve his selfish purposes by stalling for time while Zero attempted to clear him of the murder frame that Schoenling had prepared for him.

ALLYN WAS about to put the paper back on Doro Kelly's desk when his gaze shifted to another item and his colorless eyebrows drew together in an annoyed frown.

"What unmitigated moron wrote that?" he muttered more to himself than to his attractive neighbor at the next desk.

"We've one or two staff members of that mental classification," the girl said and glanced over at the boxed-in item indicated by Allyn's slightly trembling forefinger.

WORLD SCIENCE EDITOR SLEUTHS FOR RADI-ATIONS AT SCENE OF CRIME; BAGS COP
Geiger Counter Indicates Brilliance of Detective Riley

Doro tossed her dark curls. "What's wrong with it?"

"Well—" Lee Allyn swallowed. He couldn't tell her what was wrong with it. Doro Kelly swung away from her desk to face him, hands on slim hips.

"What's wrong with it, Horace Greeley?" she demanded.

He shrugged. "It's unfunny. It's supposed to be, isn't it—funny?"

"It *was* funny," she insisted. "Our own Wayland Pagget, journalism's chief contender for the title of Most Absent-minded Man, lives in the same building. Very likely he hadn't the slightest notion that Duncan Moore had been killed and that the police were investigating.

"Pagget was fiddling with this homemade Geiger counter when Riley came into the building with this Mr. Bardon in tow. Pagget says his instrument went wild. He trailed Riley and Bardon up to the Moore apartment, apparently oblivious to everything except the antics of his Geiger counter.

"He barged right onto the scene—can't you just see him?—and tried to get Ed Cavanaugh to listen to whatever it is you hear in the earphone of a Geiger counter."

Lee Allyn wasn't laughing. When Riley and Bardon had entered the Moore apartment, so had Captain Zero. Not Riley, not Bardon, but Captain Zero was responsible for the radiations detected by Wayland Pagget's Geiger counter. The brain that had planned the Moore killing wouldn't have the slightest difficulty in determining that no *visible* presence could have possibly affected Pagget's Geiger counter to such a very marked degree.

At the same time, the killer had every reason to suspect that the slaying of Duncan Moore would not escape the attention of Captain Zero. Therefore, the incident so lightly dealt with on the front page of the *World* might very well amount to a death warrant for Captain Zero, for it suggested a means of discovering his presence and exact location.

Doro Kelly stared at Lee Allyn, her lips compressed in exasperation. "Well," she said tartly, "I may be an unmitigated moron, but I do have a sense of humor."

Lee Allyn's smile was sickly. "You wrote this, huh?"

"I did." She snatched the proof sheet from his hands and went striding off toward Fairish's desk.

Allyn sighed, reached for his hat, and stood up. On his way

60

to the city hall his mind was occupied with matters of greater personal importance than Pendleville's new traffic code. From the moment that Pagget had introduced his Geiger counter, Lee Allyn had become a marked man—due to the atomic radiations from his body.

And it wasn't anything that he could do anything about. As he had tried to explain to Ed Cavanaugh, the only living person who shared his secret, "It's just something that happens periodically. You can set your watch by it. At exactly midnight, I begin to fade out of the picture. And at dawn, I appear again. I haven't any control of it at all. Some people have headaches every morning. Others have indigestion every night. But I disappear. It's an affliction, believe me. A curse."

The same high frequency rays that made his body invisible would also affect the sensitivity of the Geiger counter. In the hands of a man with enough sense to use that counter, the weapon could become the nemesis of Captain Zero—and radioactive Lee Allyn as well.

It wouldn't take long to find out. Only a split second....

CHAPTER 5
THE LEAGUE OF
FRIGHTENED MEN

THE OLD men came into the *World* offices half an hour after Lee Allyn had left. They were of assorted sizes and shapes, the lean and gnarled, the soft and plump, but they had one thing in common—fear. Confused by the activity within the city room, they huddled in the entrance while a dozen pairs of younger eyes passed unconcernedly over them.

Five old men where once there had been eight. One was blind, clinging to the arm of another, his smile incessant, his patience bovine. Doro Kelly saw them from her desk. The bald one with the curiously pointed ears she'd met on the night before at the scene of Duncan Moore's slaying.

Walter Bedlows' eyes were darkly circled from lack of sleep. He turned, now, as Fairish came out of Managing Editor Grindler's office, shook hands with the red-haired city editor and presented one of his companions—the one with the flowing black tie, the Van Dyke beard, the silvery hair.

Fairish shook hands all around and at the same time beckoned to Doro Kelly. She stood, swept up pad and pencil, and approached the group.

The gentle old thing with the flowing tie was introduced to Doro as Dale Perry, president of the Bachelors' Club. Galvin was the name of the one who was lean and gnarled. Spencer was the soft and plump, and he'd pieced out what was left of his own hair with a mouse-brown toupe. And the One Who Was Blind remained exactly that, for Fairish apparently hadn't caught the name.

"Miss Kelly," Fairish interrupted Doro's how-do-you-do's, "if you'll take these gentlemen in Grindler's office, I think you'll find enough chairs. Gentlemen, if you'll excuse me. Miss Kelly will handle the interview."

Dale Perry of the flowing tie fastened a faintly blue claw on Doro's arm and smiled his gentle smile.

"This will be a pleasure, Miss Kelly. It's not often that a group of old codgers get a chance to talk to a charming little lady like yourself."

Doro acknowledged the compliment prettily enough, wondering just where Mr. Perry got that "little lady" stuff. She led them into the deserted office of the managing editor and seated the old men in a semi-circle about the desk where they reminded her of nothing so much as pall bearers at a funeral.

But they all looked at Doro. That is, four of them did, while the One Who Was Blind smiled and tried to appear as though he were looking. He, at least, approved of her, whereas Mr. Spencer of the toupe did not. The gnarled Galvin seemed preoccupied, Walter Bedlows tolerant, while Mr. Perry regarded her as he might a child on Christmas morning.

Mr. Perry, she thought, you're going to be disappointed, because I'll neither do nor say anything cute—not in this atmosphere of crepe and lilies.

"First I'd like to get something of the history of your unique club," she began.

"What's unique about it?" Mr. Spencer asked gruffly.

"Wel-l-l—" Doro was disconcerted—"it's certainly new to me."

PERRY LAUGHED as though a child of her tender years might be expected to find something new in everything.

"It isn't new at all," said the disagreeable Mr. Spencer. "Lorenzo Tonti invented the first survivorship insurance scheme in the days of Cardinal Mazarin."

"Tonti's plan was an annuity," the Blind One corrected. "Isn't that right, Galvin? You were in insurance."

"What?" said Mr. Galvin.

"Annuity, insurance—what's the difference?"

"The point is," said Walter Bedlows, daubing at his perspiring bald head with his handkerchief, "that the last living member of this club gets the boodle—something that I pointed out to the police last night."

"Something that you took great pleasure in pointing out to the police, I have no doubt," Spencer snapped. "I, for one, resent your nasty little implication."

"My dear Spencer," Bedlows said, "there was no implication whatsoever."

"Oh, yes there was." Spencer hitched his plump body forward in the chair and his laugh was unpleasant. "The implication which you made was that one of us four was the murderer."

"I did not exclude myself," Bedlows corrected.

"By implication—yes," Spencer insisted. "The mere fact that you brought the matter to the attention of the police implies that *you* are the one above reproach. Since when has any murderer taken pains to point out his motive?"

"I did not exclude myself." Bedlows repeated, his patience wearing thin, "though of course each must answer to his own conscience."

Doro was writing furiously. This was much better than a formal interview. There was an element of drama here—the five old men quarreling among themselves, each suspicious of his neighbor, each afraid.

"Gentlemen, please," protested Mr. Perry sweetly. He pinned Doro to her chair with glinting blue eyes. "It's our little game, my dear. It amuses us. When you are much, much older perhaps you will understand that the game then is to go on living a little longer. We have simply introduced a competitive spirit and provided a trophy for the ultimate winner of the game."

"I seem to recall," the Blind One said, "our friend Perry saying that the greatest game for the hunter was

Doro Kelly

a fellow human. Isn't that right, Perry? Didn't you make that remark once after you had returned from a hunting expedition?"

Doro stared in surprise at the gentle Mr. Perry. She never would have suspected him of hunting anything beyond a lost collar button.

Perry was nodding. "Precisely my words. Since then, friend Rumpler, we have become fair game for one of us who is the hunter." He smiled his gentle smile which somehow sent a little chill coursing along Doro Kelly's spine.

"Don't you find it rather exciting, gentlemen?" Perry continued. "It is especially so for the one who is the hunter. Even I find the rôle of the bounding hare much more stimulating than a quiet game of chess with Galvin here."

They stared at their president, and after an interval of silence, the gnarled Mr. Galvin said, "No use looking at Perry. He's got plenty of money. Why would he go out after the five hundred thousand?"

Which seemed to ruffle Walter Bedlows. "And I haven't, is that it? All of you are well fixed, but I'm not. Therefore I'm the killer. Is that the idea, Galvin?"

Galvin didn't answer; he didn't even appear to have heard. The irritable Mr. Spencer picked up the gauntlet for him.

"If the shoe fits," he snapped.

It was the first direct accusation and it caused an immediate outburst of protests. Doro Kelly looked up distractedly and found that Lee Allyn was standing just within the door, a smile on his face. How long he'd been there, she had no idea. He was the most self-effacing individual she'd ever known. Lost in a crowd of five, she thought.

His smile vanished and he turned suddenly—rather nervously, it seemed to Doro—as the door on the opposite side of the corridor burst open. Wayland Pagget strode loose-jointed across the hall, pince nez glasses riding askew on the bridge of his nose. He stared in at the old men who immediately stopped their bickering.

The science editor mumbled, "Oh, pardon me," flung wildly about, and re-entered his office to slam the door.

Doro frowned quizzically at Lee Allyn who shook his head sadly and stepped out into the corridor.

"Who was that intruder, Miss Kelly?" asked Mr. Perry with a note of anxiety in his voice.

"Just one of the reporters," she informed the gentle old man. "Now, if one of you will give me a little bit of the history of your club—when it was founded and some of the background."

She let that trickle off, her gaze reaching through the open door. Something, she reflected, was wrong with Lee. She watched him turn toward the city room, come to an uncertain halt, his lips thin and his eyes uneasy.

Then he retraced his steps, paused again, this time in front of the door of the science editor. Then his slight shoulders squared and his hand went out to the knob of Pagget's door.

"WHAT GIVES with the gadget, Pagget?" The steadiness of Lee Allyn's voice was incongruous with the shakiness of his hands as he stood within the science editor's office and lighted a cigarette.

Pagget's homemade Geiger counter occupied a prominent spot on the desk along with a manuscript, now in production and doubtless on the subject of how to find uranium ore in the back yard. Pagget excitedly ripped the earphone of the instrument from his rumpled head and thrust it at Lee Allyn.

"Listen," he urged. "Exactly like last night. I didn't really think it was Riley—that was Miss Kelly's interpretation. How could it be any person, for that matter?"

"How could it?" Allyn said. He put the earphone into place,

listened a moment to the frantic ticking of the instrument. He removed the 'phone and looked at Pagget. He asked, "So what?"

"Those old men over there." Pagget jerked a nod toward Grindler's office. "Are they the ones—the suspects?"

Lee Allyn shrugged. "The victims, maybe. Thus far, the killer has done his selecting from among them. Why? What makes you think this Geiger counter has anything to do with them?"

Pagget raked at his fuzzy hair. "I don't know. But doesn't a motive suggest itself? I mean, doesn't it follow that if the Geiger counter detected emanations last night in the Duncan Moore apartment and today in the presence of Moore's fellow club members—well, doesn't it?"

"Maybe it follows," Allyn said, "but I don't. You said yourself that human beings aren't supposed to be radioactive."

"Not unless they're loaded with some radioactive chemical," Pagget said. "Say, that's an idea!"

It was, for a fact. It was the kind of an idea that made Lee Allyn feel cold all over.

He said, "What was the other idea—the one you had before you had this one? I think I'll like it better."

Pagget blinked. "Why, what other idea? Oh, yes—motive." He laughed. "Now that I give it grave consideration, it seems ridiculous. But since the police seem to be at loss for a motive, I thought perhaps that some valuable radioactive substance such as radium was at the root of it. It's priceless, you know. Suppose one of the members of the Bachelors' Club had some radium and one of the others stole it."

"That's good," Lee Allyn said. He slapped Pagget heartily on the back as though he hoped to knock Idea Number Two out of the scientist's grasshopper brain.

"You really think so?" Pagget's smile was fleeting. "But listen to this: Would anyone really steal radium? I mean the sources, even the exact amounts of the stuff in existence today are so well known, that how on earth would the thief dispose of it?"

"Well," Allyn said slowly, still trying to get Pagget to cling to the original idea, regardless of how absurd it might be, "suppose the criminal latched onto some radium that belonged to a hospital and held it for ransom. Sort of a snatch-act. Wouldn't the hospital pay a pretty penny to get it back?"

"No, no. I mean, that's a possibility, of course, but suppose that some member of the Bachelors' Club happens to be taking treatment for some disease requiring large doses of some radioactive isotope. D'you see?"

All too clearly, Lee Allyn saw.

"And," Pagget continued, "he's the person who killed Duncan Moore. Why not? Some criminals leave fingerprints. This one, due to whatever radioactive substance he has been taking, leaves emanations. He must have been there last night, all the while, hiding in Moore's apartment until the police left."

"Oh sure," Lee Allyn scoffed. He reached over and flipped off the switch of the Geiger counter. "Save your batteries," he explained. "Oh sure, the killer was hiding there. Back of the wallpaper, he was hiding. Or there's a secret room behind that phony mantel. All modern apartments have secret rooms so you can hide from the tax collector."

"I don't think this is funny," Pagget said soberly. "Damn it, Allyn, I've got something, here. I know I have."

ALLYN SAID, "Now, look, I'll tell you what we can do to prove it. When these old codgers clear out of here, I'm going to try and trail 'em. You'll have the Geiger counter on, see? If the ticking abates gradually as they leave, you'll know you've got something. Either one of them has a blob of radium burning a hole in his pocket, or he's been taking some sort of treatment. One or the other, you'll have proof that your homemade gadget isn't just acting temperamental. How about it?"

Pagget nodded enthusiastically. "I'll do that. And I'll let you know." His smile flickered. "Just suppose this were to be the first murder to be solved by a Geiger counter. What a story that would make!"

"Sure," Allyn said. "Front page stuff. I'll see you later, Walter."

Lee Allyn went out wondering how much longer he'd be able to pull the wool over Pagget's eyes, or if he had succeeded at all. He went on into the city room and to Fairish's desk where he turned in his story on the traffic ordinance. The city editor glanced at the rough.

"You might just as well do the rewrite on this, Allyn. You haven't anything better to do."

"The hell I haven't," Allyn disagreed. "I think I'm on the right end of a scoop." And as Fairish looked skeptical, Allyn continued, "It's just a rumor, but I'd like to check it. Another killing last night. No connection with the Moore job, that I can see. A small-time gun-artist named Jake Katz."

Fairish scowled. "Where'd you get this—dream it up this

morning while you were sitting on the back of your neck over there?"

"No. I can't tell you where I got the dope, but I think it's on the level."

"You checked at the morgue?"

"And everywhere else. Nobody tagged him as Jake Katz. But maybe he is."

"Maybe you're being had."

"Maybe," Allyn granted. "We'll know I wasn't when the *Sentinel* beats us with the story."

Fairish said, "Nuts! Get out on it, boy. Just turn up with something, that's all."

Allyn turned away from the desk, looked anxiously toward Grindler's office. He lighted a cigarette from the stump of the one he had been smoking and twisted the butt into the ash tray on Fairish's desk.

"Well?" Fairish looked at him curiously. "I thought you had a hot scoop."

Allyn said, "What's the hurry?" He couldn't leave the office before the five old men did because of the damned Geiger counter that Pagget was operating. "Jake Katz isn't going anywhere—not if what I hear is true."

"No," Fairish said softly, "Jake Katz isn't. But by the immortal soul of Horace Greeley, *you* are! Now, get out on it, boy, and if you don't expect to pick up your last pay envelope when you come back, bring in a story."

Lee Allyn turned, moved away slowly. He lingered at the water cooler, taking on enough water to steam a slow freight from Gotham to Frisco. He looked around, caught Fairish glaring at him, and then he filled the paper cup again. He raised the cup, gagging slightly, then lowered it as a chorus of good-byes reached his ears.

The five old men were out in the corridor now, and Doro Kelly was giving them a farewell smile. Four of them straggled off, while Perry, the arty-looking old gent, lingered to press Doro's hand. Lee Allyn moved into the corridor. Perry relinquished Doro's hand and hastened to join his comrades.

"Oh, Lee," Doro called softly, "wait a minute, will you?"

He couldn't wait. He didn't. "Gotta go," he said. "Another day, another dollar."

"But this is important, Lee."

"Bye-bye," he said, waving and walking. "Some other time."

There was a greenish light in Doro's lovely eyes. She stamped a foot. "Nuts to you, Mr. Allyn," she said quietly as he disappeared in the company of the frightened men.

In the office of the science editor, Pagget listened with bated breath to the ever-diminishing ticks from the 'phone of his Geiger counter. When they had ceased altogether, he jerked off the headpiece, stumbled over his own wastebasket getting to the door. He stuck his head out into the corridor, his glasses wobbling, came back into the room, slammed the door, and then reached for the 'phone.

CHAPTER 6
TRAIL OF THE DEAD

DOXIE MERRICK owned the Pink Mug on Jessop Street, and it was said that he'd thought of the name for his taproom one morning while shaving. Doxie's mug was pink enough, like the wizened, boneless face of a new-born baby.

Like everything else on Jessop Street, the Pink Mug wasn't much. A fine old mahogany bar with some new chrome-legged stools in front of it, and an oil-painted nude Venus-on-the-Half-Shell in a heavy gilt frame on the wall behind it. Also, there were tables for ladies.

Doxie Merrick seldom tended bar. "I got so I hate my customers," he confided to Lee Allyn. "Most of'em anyway. They makes you sick to your stummick, such trash." So he kept to his little office behind the blue painted door at the back, and deplored the state liquor laws that had compelled him to remove his brass rail.

"How'n the hell is a guy to know if he's had too much if he's on a stool and can't feel it in his legs—I ask you?"

Lee Allyn sat on a corner of the scarred desk and admitted that Doxie had something there. He liked Doxie. The ageless, pink-faced little man had frequently been an excellent source of information to him. Doxie, it was true, didn't believe in Captain Zero—"propaganda, that's what it is," he'd often said—but that was nothing against him.

"You happen to know a man by the name of Jake Katz?" Allyn asked the proprietor of the Pink Mug.

"Yeah." Doxie gave him a curdled look. "I wish I didn't. I wish I didn't know none of that crowd."

"I'm looking for his girl."

"Did you bring a truck?"

"Is she that big?"

"It ain't that she's so big as much as she's so plural." Doxie peeled a fresh cigar. "I never seen a guy with so many dames. Any particular one you had in mind? Any special shade, size or build?"

"The one he was with last night."

Doxie shook his head. "Last night, I don't know. I don't think Jake was here." He nipped the end off his cigar and set it well back on his molars. He slid far enough down in his chair so that he could reach the door with the toe of his shoe. He kicked the door open, said, "The big Irish might know," as he sighted along the line of customers at the bar. "Hey, Murph, can you come in here for a second?"

A tall, black-browed young man with hulking shoulders and a parchment yellow face slid off a bar stool and brought his beer glass to the door of Doxie's office. His hands were shaky and the beer slopped. He looked doubtfully at Lee Allyn.

"Come in and close the door, will you, Murph? I'd like you should shake hands with a friend of mine. Mr. Allyn. He's a newspaper fella," Doxie added with a note of pride.

Murphy closed the door, got his beer glass into his left hand, extended its mate to Lee Allyn. The big Irish didn't smile.

He said, "Any friend of Doxie's."

"You got the shakes today, Murph?" Doxie asked with concern.

The big man nodded. "I ought to be in bed. What's on your mind?"

"Don't Madge go out with Jake Katz some?" Doxie asked. "I think I seen her in here once or twice with him."

"Not if I know it, she don't."

"Did you know it last night?" Doxie persisted.

"I didn't. Was she?"

"We're trying to find out."

" 'We?' " The big Irish faced Lee Allyn slowly. Murph's ugly yellow face had a worried look. "What do you want with my sister, anyway?"

ALLYN SHOOK his head. "I don't know that I want anything. I'd like to know who was out with Jake Katz last night."

"I see," Murph said, as though he did. "Well, if you find out it was Madge, I wish you'd let me know. I'll warm the back of her lap for her."

Murph turned to go, but Doxie checked him with a wave of his cigar.

"What ever happened between Madge and Ned Bardon, Murph?"

The big Irish took a slow breath.

"The usual thing. You fall in love and then—" Murph shrugged—"you fall out again. Joe Melton, over at the bowling alley, said he saw Ned last night and he looked like he was doing all right. Well—" Murph raised a hand in a farewell gesture, backed out of the room, and closed the door.

"Too bad," Doxie said sadly. "Good boy, Murph."

"Malaria, isn't it?" Lee Allyn asked.

"Uh huh. He's in and out of the vets' hospital a lot. Can't hold a steady job, he's sick so much."

He broke off to massage his small, round chin thoughtfully. "You might try Mo Sipes, Lee. Him I just noticed when Murph went out. Mo Sipes and Howie Myers, over at that table near the window. Mo is Jake Katz's pal. The hatchet-faced one. Mo might be able to tell you who Jake was out with last night."

Allyn slid off the desk. "Thanks, Doxie"

Mo Sipes was the one with the hatchet profile—a thin, straight chin, a nose broken high on the bridge, gaunt and narrow and raw-boned with close-set, cold blue eyes. Howie Myers was dark and spidery, and he had curly black hair on the backs of his hands clear down to the second knuckle of his fingers. The pair shouldered around and stared at the small, impeccably neat blond man in the owlish, horn-rimmed glasses.

"You know Jake Katz?" Lee Allyn addressed the question to Mo Sipes.

Mo Sipes blew down his nose, looked at Howie Myers.

"Do we know Jake Katz, he asts," Howie said.

"What's with Jake?" Mo Sipes asked Allyn.

"I'm trying to find out who Jake was out with last night," Allyn asked.

"Some broad." Mo Sipes laughed.

"Yeah, some broad." Howie Myers laughed.

The pair looked at each other and laughed in unison. Mo Sipes pulled a thick, nickel-plated watch out of his pants pocket and consulted it. Howie Myers pushed back his cuff and looked at his watch.

And then, oddly, they both looked at each other's watches—quick, comparative glances that might have escaped a less astute person than Lee Allyn. It was exactly twelve noon. They both pushed back from the table and stood up—the tall, slow Mo Sipes and the short, quick Howie Myers.

"Excuse us, buddy," Mo Sipes said.

"Yeah, maybe some other time," Howie Myers said.

They crowded forward, and Lee Allyn backed. Then they turned and went out of the door of the Pink Mug to climb into a black two-door sedan that was parked at the curb.

There was something in the air. It smelled. Lee Allyn thought, Well here goes nothing. He moved to the screen door, paused, watched the sedan roll away from the curb. Then he shoved out through the screen and sprinted toward the *World* staff car parked four doors down the street.

TWELVE O'CLOCK noon, and Ned Bardon came out of the washroom in the offices of Earhart & Cline, Investment Brokers. He'd damped and combed his blond hair, had straightened his tie, and had given his tan oxfords a brisk touch-up with a pocket-sized polishing kit he carried.

As he moved across the front office, he whistled softly a bar or two from some tune that happened to come into his head at the moment. The middle-aged brunette at the receptionist's desk looked up and smiled.

"Mr. Cline would like you to step into his office for a minute, Mr. Bardon, before you go to lunch."

Bardon said, "Right." He turned, crossed the room to enter Mr. Cline's office. "You want to see me, sir?"

Marvin Cline nodded. He was in his middle sixties, a straight-backed figure of a man in a conservative blue suit. He had a thin, sallow face and one of the most persistent peptic ulcers that any fluoroscope had ever discovered.

Nervous movements of his thin hands swept papers into a manila folder which he closed and placed aside, uncovering a copy of the early edition of the *World*. He tapped the column which dealt with the Duncan Moore slaying and his hard eyes drilled Ned Bardon's face.

"Don't like this sort of thing, Bardon," he said.

Ned Bardon said with feeling, "And neither do I, sir. It's the most unpleasant experience I've ever had."

"So I should imagine," Cline said dryly. "It isn't the best publicity for the firm, either. Oh, I realize you kept Earhart & Cline out of it," he added as Bardon opened his mouth to protest, "but your connection with our house is rather well known." Cline cleared his throat. "Most unfortunate, of course. Not a thing in the world you could do about it. But in the future, if you find yourself in any situation which you think might not lend any luster to the name of Earhart & Cline, I wish you'd contact me at once. I might have kept your name out of the papers entirely had you let me know. Not—" he smiled brief-ly—"that you are apt to find yourself in similar circumstances again."

"I sincerely hope not, sir," Bardon said.

"Your record, as a whole, is good. Excellent, I might say."

"Thank you, sir."

One of the gray hands on the desk moved slightly in a gesture of dismissal, and then as Ned Bardon was half turned toward the door, Mr. Cline's dry voice spoke again.

"By the way, did the late Duncan Moore ever say anything to you about wishing to lay hands on some shares of Reynox Preferred?"

A slight frown shadowed Ned Bardon's blue eyes. "No, sir."

"The reason I ask," Cline continued, "is that a day or so prior to his—uh—death, Mr. Moore called me on the 'phone, made some inquiries regarding the Reynox firm. It seemed odd that he should question me about the matter, inasmuch as you were handling his account."

Ned Bardon stared thoughtfully at the sunlit window. "It is odd. Mr. Moore always impressed me as being very well informed in regard to the market. He ought to have known that no Reynox is being offered." His eyes returned to Mr. Cline. "You're sure it *was* Mr. Moore?"

Cline shrugged. "It might not have been. That's probably the answer." His smile flickered. "Lunching with Miss Gerard, I presume?"

"Right," Ned Bardon said, resenting this interest in his private affairs.

"Charming young woman," Cline commented. "Sorry to have detained you."

"That's quite all right, sir." Ned Bardon stepped briskly to the door, went out, and was closing the door behind him when he heard the voice of the receptionist.

"There's a gentleman here to see you, Mr. Bardon."

NED BARDON turned. His step faltered slightly, the muscles of his mouth tightened.

"Oh, yes," he said, recovering quickly, and continued on toward the corridor. "Now, about that bathroom drain," he began, his eyes fixed squarely on those of the enormous man in the rumpled white suit who rose from the chair nearest the door.

Fat Paul Schoenling chuckled as he followed Ned Bardon out into the corridor.

"Don't ever come here again," Ned Bardon said out of the side of his mouth as the fat man came abreast of him.

Schoenling laughed aloud. "And do I remind you of a plumber, my dear sir!"

"Shut up, damn it!" Ned Bardon was hurrying toward the elevators as though hoping to outstrip his huge and wheezy companion.

Schoenling nipped the young man's coat sleeve in his puffy fingers. "Perhaps we should return to your office for our little chat."

Ned Bardon made a short, flat-handed gesture. "Like hell," he said softly. "Take the elevator. I'll meet you in two minutes in the bar around the corner."

He jerked away from the fat man and continued to the mouth of the stairway. There he glanced back. Schoenling stood in the little group in front of the elevator shaft. He wasn't even looking in Ned Bardon's direction.

Sure of yourself, aren't you? Ned Bardon thought with a slight smile as he started down the stairs. And then his mind leaped ahead to Ann. She'd be waiting for him in the foyer of the Old Colony Restaurant—waiting, watching the clock, worrying.

He hadn't told Ann of Schoenling nor of the visit from Captain Zero on the night before. He'd have to tell her, he supposed. She really ought to know and understand the situation in all its complexities.

For a moment he gravely considered giving Schoenling the slip. But what would be gained? An hour or so, perhaps, and then Schoenling would find him. And perhaps he'd be even more brash about making his demands.

There was nothing to do except follow through with his part of the agreement. If he could twist the thing to his advantage, so much the better. It still represented his only way out of the mess he'd got into on Jessop Street.

Fat Paul Schoenling was just easing himself into one of the tight little booths at the back of the Golden Pheasant Bar when Ned Bardon passed through the front door. He strode to the back of the room, slid in opposite Schoenling, and said, "Whiskey sour," to the hovering waitress. As soon as the girl had disappeared, he looked squarely into Schoenling's piggy eyes.

"Shoot."

"Oh, it's not that bad," Schoenling said, chuckling. "We've not come to shooting yet. I merely want your decision. Do you dispose of these securities of mine—I use the possessive rather loosely, eh?—or do I dispose of you in the manner outlined last night?"

Ned Bardon drew his lower lip across his teeth. He nodded slowly. "On one condition," he added.

"You're not in a position to bargain, my dear fellow."

"I think I am," Ned Bardon insisted. "I think you need me almost as much as I don't need you. There are angles in this business which I know and which you couldn't possibly know. If I've got to get into this thing, I want to get in with both feet. I'll want your complete confidence and a fair share of whatever comes our direction."

SCHOENLING'S EYEBROWS went up. "My dear chap! That's a tall order. Why should I even consider it?"

"Because I'm in a spot to throw a lot of business your way. Because I have information at my fingertips you couldn't touch in a million years. Because I've got the confidence of a lot of Very Important People."

Schoenling pursed his small mouth. "Perhaps. Perhaps not. Understand, I'm not the only party involved. This shall have to be gone into rather carefully. Suppose I see you this evening sometime."

"When?" Ned Bardon wanted to know.

"Oh, sometime." The fat man chuckled. "I'm a person of sudden entrances, as you know."

"Right." Ned Bardon stood.

"You've got a drink coming," Schoenling reminded him.

"Drink it," Ned Bardon flung over his shoulder as he headed for the street door.

It was 12:15 when he entered the Old Colony Restaurant and saw Ann Gerard waiting on the maple settle in the pine paneled foyer, her eyes alert, the fingers of her white gloved hands tightly knitted in her lap. She wore a white eyelet dress and carried a white cartwheel hat, and the shimmering mass of her glorious red hair fell in waves to her shoulders.

She saw him, then, in the crowd, and she lowered her satiny eyelids for a moment and sighed out a long-pent breath. The tautness went out of her face. Her lips curved into a serene smile, and he kissed them with his eyes.

"Worried?" he whispered as he took her arm and steered her through the wide-cased opening into the dining room.

"Awfully, darling. But not now."

The hostess showed them to a table in a secluded spot in the quaint room. For a brief interval they held hands across the checkered cloth, proud of their love, sure.

How sure? he wondered suddenly. "What was the idea last night," he asked, "putting that old disk on the phonograph?"

"Oh, you found that out, did you?" she asked archly.

"Uh huh. And what was the idea?"

She smiled. "It seemed like a very good one, darling. Did she really love you that much—this Madge?"

"So you played it through, did you?"

Her laughter tinkled. "Naturally. Oughtn't a woman to be curious? What is Madge like, darling? Is she as lovely as her voice?"

"Forget about her," he said.

"She sent that record to you when you were in the South Pacific, didn't she?"

"Forget about her," he repeated. "I have." He released her hands and picked up the menu. He frowned at the menu for a long time without reading a word of it. And then his eyes met Ann's across the table.

"Is anything—wrong, Ned?"

He flattened the menu and picked at the corner of it. Finally, he nodded and looked up.

"A couple of things," he said, "are wrong."

Pallor edged beneath her rouge.

CHAPTER 7
THE BIG KNOCKOVER

LEE ALLYN'S *World* staff car pulled over to the curb in front of the Hildebrand Apartments on Broadmoor Avenue where, little more than twelve hours ago, old Duncan Moore had faced his slayer with only a harmless patented shooting device for protection.

Half a block ahead of Allyn, the two-door sedan which he had followed all the way across town had parked in front of the corner drugstore. Howie Myers sauntered across the sidewalk and entered a side door in the drugstore building while the hatchet-faced Mo Sipes slumped behind the wheel and lit a cigarette. Nothing about their actions would hare excited suspicion, yet why had Mo and Howie compared watches back at the Pink Mug? Wasn't that an indication of plans requiring split-second scheduling?

Allyn's formless hunch persisted, and his attitude in the press car was that of a man who lounges on the point of a pin. He took off his glasses and wiped perspiration from their lenses. The noon hour hush had settled over the blazing street, and the thin, clear voice of a child that drifted through the open window of the car startled Allyn.

"Look, Mummy! Bird caught up there. He caught, he caught!"

Allyn put on his glasses and discovered a little girl in an abbreviated sun suit playing quietly on the square of lawn in front of the apartment building. She stood, bare toes wriggling in the grass, and pointed up toward the eaves.

The child's mother, as coolly clad in shorts and halter bra, sat in the shade of a stiff little maple. She looked up through dark sun-glasses and laughed at the child's excited wonderment.

"The bird is building a nest, darling," she explained. "You watch."

"Now him loose, Mommy!" The child clapped tiny hands. "Watch out, birdie, you get caught again." She uttered an excited squeal. "I told you, I told you! No—" with a note of disappointment—"him loose again. See, Mommy?"

Lee Allyn glanced up at the bird fluttering around the furled awning over an east window on the third floor. Now and then it would dart and snap at a dangling bit of thread in an effort to pull it loose.

"The bird isn't caught, honey," the mother explained to the little girl. "There's a raveling or something on that awning, and the bird is trying to get it for its nest."

"Why him want a nawning, Mommy?"

"Not the awning, silly—the raveling."

"Why him want the rabeling?"

"To make the nest strong. And you ask too many questions."

A child at play, the mother lounging in the shade, the bird

building a nest, the street shimmering in the noonday sun and beneath this placid surface the undercurrent of violence. Up ahead, a car door slammed, and Allyn's attention was drawn to Mo Sipes crossing the sidewalk to enter the same door through which Howie Myers had passed a few minutes before.

Allyn sidled across the cushions, opened the door, and got out. The little girl on the lawn of the apartment building looked at him curiously.

"Hi. What's your name?"

"Lee." Allyn's smile quirked and disappeared. He moved on up the street and, when he came abreast of the door into the drugstore building, he noticed that Mo Sipes had climbed a steep flight of stairs. There were signs inside the door indicating that the offices of A.F. Martin, M.D., and P.S. Lopez, D.D.S., were located on the second floor.

As he went up the stairs, it occurred to Lee Allyn that this didn't have to mean anything beyond the possibility that both Mo and Howie might be drug addicts like their erstwhile pal, Jake Katz; that they might have traveled all the way across town to pick up a shot from some renegade doctor.

The corridor at the head of the stairs seemed dingy after the bright glare of the street. To the left, Allyn saw the tall figure of Mo Sipes in a waiting room, standing in front of a closed door, his back toward Allyn. Mo seemed to be staring at the card that read, "Doctor Not In. Will Return At—" and the hands of the pasteboard clock were set at 2:30.

Allyn took three steps toward the door of the doctor's waiting room. Behind him was a stir of sound—the crack of a floorboard, an indrawn breath. He half turned.

That was when the building fell in on him.

HOWIE MYERS slapped the palm of his left hand with the braided leather blackjack he held in his right. He looked down at the slight, very pale young man who had collapsed at his feet.

He said, "Aw right, nosy."

Mo Sipes came out of the deserted waiting room. Uncertainty rode the frown that gathered above his close-set eyes. He pursed his lips.

"What the hell you think we're going to do with him?"

The dark spidery man shrugged. "Leave him where he's at."

Mo Sipes thoughtfully rubbed his thin jaw. "Huh uh."

"Why not?" Howie argued in a whisper. "What's wrong with a guy passin' out in a doctor's office?"

Mo looked as though there was plenty wrong. "He was tailin' us. How'd he get wise? What's he wanna know about Jake for?" Mo stuck out the toe of his shoe and nudged Lee Allyn under the ribs, but the pale young man didn't seem to mind.

"He'll keep," Howie said and returned his blackjack to the tight slot of his right hip pocket.

"We got to kill the nosy son," Mo Sipes said.

"Here?" Howie laughed uneasily.

Mo shook his head. "We take him with us." He crouched, hauled the unconscious man into a sitting position. He swept up the battered straw hat and soused it on Lee Allyn's head. Then he brought the reporter's limp right arm up and across his own shoulders.

"You mean we drag him out into the street, for cripe-sakes?" The sweat prickled out on Howie's forehead. His dark eyes were big and round.

"Uh huh," Mo replied. "Get his other wing and hoist him to his feet. What's wrong with our pal got a dose of too much sun, see?"

Howie grinned as he got down on the other side of the reporter. Trust Mo to think up something smart. Mo was a guy who could talk his way out of anything.

Together they lifted the limp figure into an upright position and lugged him to the head of the stairs. Blinding light from the street struck Howie across the eyes, and against it he saw the silhouette of a woman on her way up the stairs.

She paused, looking up, her rouged lips apart. Howie's knees caved and his tongue seemed to swell until it filled his mouth and throat. The woman was wearing white. A nurse, maybe—nobody's dummy.

"Our friend collapsed on the street," Mo Sipes was saying easily. "Too much sun. It'll do it every time. The doc isn't in, is he, Miss?"

The girl came up three more steps. She shook her head. "Not until 2:30, and it's sometimes later than that." Her eyes studied the sagging figure between the two men. "You ought to get him to a hospital. Bring him into the waiting room, and I'll call an ambulance."

"Thanks," Mo said, "but we got a car downstairs. We'll take him there ourselves. I don't think he'd like it if he came to and found we run out on him."

The woman in white hurried to the top of the stairs to clear the way. Mo and Howie started down with Lee Allyn between them.

There was nobody on the sidewalk within a hundred yards of them except a little girl in a sun suit playing on the lawn in front of the Hildebrand Apartments. Howie got the door of the two-door sedan open, pushed the seat-back forward. They lifted and pushed and let go and the slight young man fell at full-length on the floor of the car.

"Go 'round and cover him up with the robe," Mo said softly in Howie's ear. "We treat him for shock, see? Keep him warm. If he smothers to death, he won't talk, will he?"

HOWIE STUMBLED around the car, opened the door on the other side. He yanked the robe off the back seat and tumbled it over Lee Allyn's face. A bead of sweat formed at the end of Howie's nose.

On the curb side of the car, Mo was cramping the unconscious man's legs into the car to pull the robe down over them. Howie stepped back and slammed the door. Mo pushed the seat back and climbed in under the wheel while Howie went around the back of the car.

He looked in both directions. Nobody watching except the kid in the sun suit on the apartment lawn. Howie got in and Mo turned over the engine.

"Geez!" Howie said and wiped the sweat off his face on the sleeve of his navy blue coat.

"You're sure he'll keep?" Mo Sipes asked as he turned into Inland Street.

"Like meat in a deep freeze. Only I'm not so sure Fat Paul is gonna like this."

"To hell with Fat Paul," Mo said contemptuously. His hard dark eyes scouted along the sidewalk, along the fronts of the various shops. Two doors from the Inland Street branch of the Pendleville National Bank, on the steps of a hamburg joint that probably wasn't doing too much business, he spotted a stocky figure in a tan suit and straw snap-brim.

"There's Monk," Mo said. "I guess everything is okay. All the boys staked out." He swung the car into a parking spot near the front of the squat concrete and glass-brick building that housed the branch office of the bank. He said to Howie, "You get over. Remember the Venetian blind. When it drops, turn her over."

Mo Sipes cut the ignition switch, opened the left hand door, and got out. Howie slid under the wheel, glanced over his shoulder and down at the swathed figure on the floor.

"He'll keep," Howie assured himself. He got out cigarettes and lighted one. His hands were rock steady. Everything was under control. In the rear vision mirror, he saw Mo saunter toward the hamburg joint.

Then Monk Lewis came down the steps, a wide grin on his face, stuck out his hand to Mo. Howie chuckled. This was better than a movie—Mo and Monk standing there in broad daylight, talking like a couple of business acquaintances. Monk even had a briefcase, with maybe a heater in it, and Howie would have given a couple of bucks to know what they were talking about. Baseball, maybe. Or about women that passed them on the sidewalk.

I hope it comes off soon, Howie thought. I hope it comes off before this guy in back starts kicking. Except for him, it would be a perfect set-up.

A short, dark man with scar on his chin, wearing blue slacks and a yellow sports shirt, approached the bank building from the east. That was Little Al Gomez, and under the loosely hanging tail of his shirt he'd have a belly gun. Little Al didn't look at Howie, didn't appear to notice Monk and Mo. Little Al simply pushed open the screen door of the bank and went in.

Howie's belly muscles rippled with suppressed laughter as the Jessop Street mob converged upon the bank. Nick Kalapolis and Duke Laymon were moving diagonally across the street. Mo and Monk sauntering along the sidewalk.

And then the laughter went out of him as a black car bearing the blue insignia of the Pendleville Police Department slid into the curb directly behind the car in which Howie was seated.

Howie momentarily shut his eyes as though to hide, ostrich fashion. The only occupant of the police car—a tall, middle-aged man in plainclothes—got out, paused to flip his cigarette into the gutter, and then entered the bank. Fat Paul Schoenling had told the Jessop Street boys to expect a cop, but he hadn't said it would be Lieutenant-of-Detectives Beckridge.

Now Mo and Monk were at the door of the bank, pausing briefly to exchange glances. And then they followed Beckridge into the building.

Howie held his breath. It had to happen fast, before Beckridge got much of a chance to look around. Fast and smooth and with a minimum—an absolutely minimum—of noise, Fat Paul had said. Howie flung his right arm up over the back of the seat, half turned to the right to watch the door of the bank, to wait for the signal. Fear lumped coldly within him.

INSIDE THE bank, Lieutenant Beckridge was shaking hands with a florid-faced man from the Federal Estate Tax office. The tax official's name was Jantz.

"And this is Mr. Cline, the executor of the Duncan Moore estate," the tax official said.

Cline, of the firm of Earhart and Cline, thin, sallow, of erect bearing in spite of his sixty-odd years, slipped thin dry fingers into Beckridge's hand.

He said, "How do you do, Lieutenant? Shall, we get at our business immediately?"

The gunmen had counted on that delay for introductions. Mo and Monk had moved ahead of the trio to the door in the partition that separated the manager's office and the safety deposit vaults from the rest of the single large room. That was according to plan. Beckridge, or whoever the cop happened to be, would be less likely to recognize Mo and Monk from the rear view than if he met them head-on. Monk had tapped on the door. The branch manager had left his desk, had worked the trick lock, and was now standing across the threshold, smiling, his eyes moving from Monk to Mo.

Mo said, "My partner and I are starting a little business in this neighborhood. We'd like to open a joint checking account." He managed it easily, even with the breath of the law on the back of his neck.

The branch manager bowed slightly, stepped back from the door, and Mo and Monk entered.

"If you'll just step over to my desk," the manager said. Then, looking beyond Mo and Monk, "Ah, good afternoon, gentlemen. The Moore box, isn't it? Miss Nellis." This to the middle-aged lady in one of the tellers' cages.

The manager left Beckridge, Cline, and the tax official to Miss Nellis, turned and approached his desk where Mo and Monk were standing, their backs warily toward Lieutenant Beckridge. Little Al Gomez was at Miss Nellis' window, his left hand extending a twenty dollar bill beneath the brass bars, his right poised at the hem of his dangling shirt; inches from the gun.

He flicked a glance to the left. A woman in gray slacks was just leaving the next window, tucking her pass book into her purse. Next up was Nick Kalapolis. A man wearing dungarees and a truck driver's cap was at the third window with Duke Laymon directly behind him. The Duke looked nervous, Little Al thought.

Little Al's eyes returned to Miss Nellis. She and the cop and the old duck and the beefy man were grouped about a bracketed desk on the side of the room near the vault. Miss Nellis was filling out a slip which she passed to the old duck to sign. From the manager's desk, in the opposite corner, Mo Sipes' voice reached Little Al's ears.

"How long's the bank been in business, Mr. Cole? We'd like to know something about you folks, naturally."

Stalling for time—that was what Mo Sipes was doing. They wouldn't move until Miss Nellis pulled the Moore box out of the vault. She was going into the vault now, her keys jingling like sleigh bells. The old duck was still at the bracket desk, talking in low tones to the man with the beefy face.

And the cop was a little apart from the other two, his tongue searching the inside of his mouth, sucking a tooth, not looking at anybody in particular. He made Little Al jumpy, nevertheless, the damned cop did. Once his gray eyes touched Little Al's face, and Little Al brought the twenty dollar bill up quickly to hide the scar on his chin while his right hand went in under his shirt and closed on the butt of his belly gun.

But the gray eyes moved on. Lieutenant Beckridge's mind was actually miles away. His mind was out in the country, that little place he and Myrtle had looked at yesterday evening after he'd gone off duty. It wasn't a fancy place at all—a white house on a green knoll with two old locust trees on either side and a well with a hand pump right at the front door.

They were maybe going to buy that place. Then, in eight years, when he retired, they'd have it paid for and could move in. They'd put in a bathroom, a pressure pump for the well so they could have running water. And Myrtle could raise chickens and he—well, he wanted to grow roses. A funny thing for a cop to want to do, maybe, but that was it.

You took cuttings and stuck them in sand and the roots came miraculously. And you could have a greenhouse, maybe sell the blooms to florists. There was money in it, if you had the time and the patience, and Beckridge had both—a good ten years before him, anyway, after he retired.

BECKRIDGE WAS dimly aware that Miss Nellis was coming out of the vault with a long, crackle-finished brown metal box in her hand. Beckridge was also dimly aware of other things that happened simultaneously.

For one, the branch bank manager seemed to have tipped back too far in his chair. He'd fallen to the floor with a crash. And behind Beckridge, on the other side of the partition, somebody laughed—a high, hysterical kind of laugh that broke off abruptly.

And then Beckridge was aware, no longer dimly, that he was in trouble clear up to his neck. Two tellers were backing away from their respective windows and there were two guns in steady hands eyeing them through the bars. At the third window, the man in the yellow sports shirt wheeled, brandished a heavy automatic at the five or six customers lined up back of the windows, and legged toward the front door.

Two men turned from the manager's desk with the manager now on his feet, his hands over his head. And Mo Sipes—Beckridge instantly recognized the hatchet-faced man—was swinging toward Beckridge. Mo had a long-barreled gun, or it was merely of average length with a silencer attached.

"This is a stick-up!" Mo's voice rang out. "Anybody wants it, gets it!"

Beckridge didn't want it. He had wanted only to serve out the rest of his tenure as a police officer with the same average luck which had thus far blessed him. He had wanted, then, to retire to the little place in the country and potter among his rose cuttings. He wanted no part of what Mo Sipes had to offer, and yet Beckridge did exactly what was expected of him, automatically and without thinking.

He went for his gun, his hand a streak from right thigh to shoulder. It was fast, but he must have known that it wouldn't be fast enough, that he couldn't beat taut nerves on a triggering finger. There was the *splot* of sound from the silenced gun, the physical impact of the slug, the wisping smoke and its acrid smell on his nostrils as the floor rushed up to meet him.

"Anybody else?"

That was Mo Sipes' generous offer. Little Al Gomez heard it from his position beside the front door. There was a man moving unconcernedly along the sidewalk, and as he turned toward the bank, Little Al slammed the door in the patron's face and let the Venetian blind fall—the usual sign that the bank was closed and also a signal to Howie Myers in the getaway car.

The surprised bank patron peered through the slots of the blind, his mouth agape, wheeled suddenly and dashed out into the street and toward the drugstore on the opposite side.

"Step on it, you son!" Little Al sang out. He swung around, waving his rod, and his oaths whip-lashed the frightened customers who were being herded into the rear of the bank by Duke Laymon. Like sheep, they were.

One woman bleated like a sheep, and Little Al snarled at her to shut her mouth. She went on through the door, pushing the man in front of her. There Monk and Mo took over, and the sheep filed into the bank vault.

The manager, the tellers, the stiff-backed old duck, the man with the beefy face—all the sheep went into the vault, and Monk swung the huge door shut. There was only the cop on the floor, his eyes squeezed shut, his breath coming with a hideous liquid sound.

Little Al said again, "Step on it, you son!" He could hear Howie jazzing the throttle of the getaway car and it made him nervous. He glanced back over his shoulder, saw Mo scooping bonds out of the Moore box and stuffing them into a sack. He saw Duke Laymon, Nick Kalapolis, and Monk Lewis stuffing the long green into sacks from the tills.

And then somebody—it could have been any one of them—touched the wrong thing in his haste, or stepped on a button, or caught a sleeve on a switch. Whatever it was an electric gong cut loose.

Then it was like quitting time in a sweat-shop. The four men behind the partition took what they had and jammed the connecting door. They pushed on through to the street door held wide open by Little Al who cursed them for a bunch of leaden-legged stumblebums. They went out into the blazing sun, Little Al last of all. And Howie was sliding the clutch on the getaway car so that it crept along the curb.

Then, with only three on board, he let the clutch slam in, put the juice to it, rocketed forward, with Little Al and Nick Kalapolis left stranded on the curb.

NICK KALAPOLIS turned confusedly and bumped into Little Al. Little Al gave Howie a name, clutched at Nick, waved his gun at the nearest car. The copper's car. Sure. The copper maybe didn't take the key out. The copper was maybe thinking about something else and didn't lock his car. Little Al gained the door, got it open, saw the key in the ignition lock. Where there had been only hopelessness the flicker of an eyelash before, now relief spread through him like the warmth from a double slug of raw whiskey. Nick Kalapolis shoved him from behind.

"Get going, for cripesake!"

Little Al got going.

Inside the bank, Lieutenant Beckridge got up. He didn't know how he did it, but he did. He got up and started to climb up what had become a steeply inclined floor. He made it, somehow, to the top, where there was a door.

He made it through the door, numb fingers grasping the butt of his under-arm gun to free it from its harness. Then there was more floor, all up hill, another door that he staggered toward, thinking, After this, another door, and another. And another.

He was suddenly in the street. The world was full of sound and motion. Pelting feet and screaming rubber. Streaking cars and screaming people. And from the dizzy kaleidoscope that whirled about him, he picked one familiar object—his car with the blue shield on its door accelerating down the street.

Beckridge raised his gun laboriously and fired. High, he thought, way, way too high. His gun arm started down, kept on going down until it weighed a ton and dangled helplessly at his side. He could not move it at all.

Look up, he told himself. The sun is shining.

He didn't even feel the impact of the slug that Nick Kalapolis put into him from the speeding police car. Beckridge didn't feel it because he was dead before he hit the pavement.

A ROAR of sound filled Lee Allyn's ears. His eyes sprang open on darkness that was like black velvet but smelled more like reclaimed wool. The knuckles of his right hand were up against his mouth, pressed there by the confining dark. He clawed feebly and a thread of light came down from somewhere above his skull and showed him the texture of the cloth that was smothering him. Rough napped wool.

As he fought it away from his face, he became aware of a sickening sense of motion that seemed a part of him, as the roar was a part of him. He closed his eyes until the nausea abated somewhat. And then pain drove deep into his brain, coming in throbs.

Inches in front of him rubber matting slanted upward. The foot-rest of the rear compartment of a car, he thought. Against the foot-rest was a narrow canvas sack, its mouth gaping open. With every lurch of the speeding car, a narrow folded piece of greenish paper inched from the open mouth of the sack. A bond or stock certificate—something like that.

And then he began to remember Mo and Howie.

Mo's voice said, "For cripesake, what's the hurry?"

Howie's said, "The damned cop."

There was harsh laughter and somebody said. "That's no cop—that's Little Al."

"In the cop's car?"

"Sure inna cop's car. You should see the cop."

"Yeah, you should see the cop."

"Geez, that's funny. Geez, that's one on me!" And Howie started to laugh.

The car swept around a wide curve and the stock certificate slipped a little farther from the mouth of the bag—far enough so that Lee Allyn's near-sighted eyes could make out some of the ornate printing. The word Reynox—he saw that much before somebody put a foot down on his neck. He gasped audibly.

"Hey," Mo Sipes said, "our boy's awake."

"So put him to sleep."

"So put him to sleep, the man said."

A heel—it might have been a wrench, a blackjack, or anything—slammed to the back of Lee Allyn's skull. Then there was no more roar, no sickening motion, no pain, no anything at all.

CHAPTER 8
THE RADIOACTIVE MAN

NIGHTMARE EMERGED from darkness. There was a man by the name of Reynox who was selling Geiger counters from a pitchman's box. Reynox had a vaguely familiar voice, but Lee Allyn couldn't see his face. He kept inching through the crowd trying to see the pitchman's face, but then Reynox didn't have any face—just a blur of white beneath the shadowy brim of his hat.

The Geiger counters were different than any that Allyn had ever seen. They neither ticked nor flashed nor had micrometers. They had a little doll on top of the case, and the more Lee Allyn looked at the tiny image more nearly it resembled Doro Kelly.

It won't work, he thought in his dream. He wanted to see if it would work, and yet he knew he oughtn't to stick around to find out. He ought to run. He couldn't run. He couldn't do anything but watch the bewitching little dolls on top of the Geiger counters. And then the faceless Reynox turned a switch on the side of one of the counters. A miniature Doro Kelly raised her arm like a pointer and spun around.

She said, "So I'm an unmitigated moron, am I? Well, *you're* Captain Zero!" And her blue eyes turned green and she pointed directly at Lee Allyn in the crowd.

Then he could run. His feet pelted the sidewalk, his legs were a blur, yet every time he looked back over his shoulder, the faceless pitchman with the Geiger counter was just behind him, moving at a leisurely pace, sure of himself, the miniature Doro Kelly pointing relentlessly at the frantic, panting and hopeless Lee Allyn....

Then reality emerged from nightmare. The voice that he had associated with the name Reynox—where the name, if it was a name, had come from, he didn't know—was actually speaking as though in the next room. Allyn kept his eyes tightly closed, the frightening shadows of the nightmare still upon him. He felt as though he had been sick for a long, long time.

"You purchased the Geiger counters?" That was "Reynox."

"Yes, my dear colleague." And that, unmistakably, was the fat man Schoenling. "I quite exhausted the stock of Central Scientific Supply. Told them I was organizing an expedition to prospect for uranium ore, exactly as you told me to do. I have them in my car right now, though what earthly good they are, I haven't the remotest idea."

"I believe they can be used to detect the presence of Captain Zero."

Schoenling burst out laughing. "My dear chap, don't tell

me you take stock in that newspaper clap-trap. Invisible man, indeed! Captain Zero, you say. I've never met the gentleman."

"Don't be too sure that you won't," the other said dryly. "But this other matter you mentioned—this difficulty, I believe you said."

"Oh, yes. Difficulty with my securities outlet."

"What sort?"

"The young bounder wants to get into the act," Schoenling said, chuckling. "Wants to be taken into our confidence. Wants a split of the spoils, I've no doubt."

"Well?"

"Perhaps I ought to explain the situation somewhat," Schoenling continued. "This young man is a person of character, employed by the local firm of Earhart and Cline. Actually, he's between the devil and the deep blue sea. Do you follow me?"

"No."

"I have him framed," Schoenling said, "to be perfectly frank. Framed for murder. Evidence which I can produce at will. That's why the young man is inclined somewhat to be in a—shall we say, a cooperative mood? But now he refuses to dispose of these securities unless we make him a partner."

LYING AT full length on what impressed him as an extremely hard floor, Lee Allyn silently congratulated Ned Bardon on his courage and resourcefulness. And then Allyn listened to the voice which he unaccountably associated with the name "Reynox."

"Suppose you appear to take him into your confidence to a

certain extent and then show him this evidence you say you have. Is it something concrete?"

"Oh dear me, yes!" Fat Paul said. "Charmingly concrete. A woman. An eye-witness, in fact, who's quite willing to swear that our young man committed murder and then disposed of the body."

"Good. Show him exactly where he stands. Show him you mean business, that he's in no position to bargain. As long as he can dispose of the securities advantageously...."

The rest was lost to Lee Allyn's ears, muffled beneath a swiftly increasing roar of sound that included the recognizable chug and clank of a locomotive that shook the building on its foundation. Allyn opened his eyes a little way. There was sickly yellow illumination. His throbbing head and his right cheek rested on a section of filthy straw matting that covered the floor.

Tilting back in a chair, his feet on a radiator beneath an open window, was the hatchet-faced Mo Sipes. An up-draft of hot air sucked the smell of coal smoke into the room. Allyn rolled his eyes up as far as possible and could just see the corner of a door that opened on the adjoining room. In there the two men were speaking. Now, as the roar of the train abated somewhat he caught a few words from "Reynox" that caused the cold sweat to break out all over Allyn's body.

"... bring up one of the Geiger counters, and I'll show you how it works."

And it'll work, Allyn thought, groaning inwardly. It'll work just peachy with me lying here practically on top of it. Good lord, if the time was just right—

He moved his left arm slightly, brought his hand up to rest on his left hip. His frightened gaze shifted to Mo Sipes seated in the chair in front of the window. Mo hadn't moved, continued to stare out into the dark through the open window, his sharp profile toward Lee Allyn.

Allyn's hand crept over his hip, turned slightly. Looking down his nose, he could see the dial of his wrist watch. The time was 10:30. An hour and a half until midnight, the zero hour. No possible hope of delaying the Geiger counter demonstration that "Reynox" planned for Schoenling's benefit. No hope at all from any conceivable source.

Allyn heard Schoenling's heavy tread as the latter crossed the adjoining room, went out a door, and down a flight of steps. "Reynox" would show him how it worked, and the indicator would clearly show the presence of radioactive emanations. To Lee Allyn's frantic mind, it was only a short jump from there to conclusion that Allyn was Captain Zero.

And then he was dead. As good as dead.

Allyn's short indrawn breath was audible. Across the room, Mo Sipes took his feet off the radiator and stood up. He stood almost at attention, one corner of his thin mouth caught up in a smile, not looking at Allyn at all, his close-set eyes on the door.

"Yeah, boss?" Mo Sipes said with a kind of fawning eagerness.

ALLYN ROLLED his eyes upward, still without moving his head. And there was "Reynox" standing just within the room—"Reynox" who, just as in the nightmare version, hadn't any face.

Beneath the soft black hat he wore a hood of black sateen the ends of which were tucked down neatly inside the collar of a long black coat. Through narrow slots in the hood, the eyes that met Lee Allyn's glinted coldly. Allyn, out of sheer bravado, was the first to speak though his voice was faint and shaky.

"It's one of two things: You either have a hair lip you're afraid somebody will notice, or you're rehearsing for your own execution. Is that what it is—a killing?"

"For yours, I think," the muffled voice returned.

Mo Sipes slapped a lean thigh. "You're a card, boss!" Then, as the hooded face turned in his direction, Mo's laughter trickled off into silence.

"Who is he?" the man in black demanded.

Mo looked uneasily toward Allyn and then back to the other. "Some nosy con," he said. "He was tailing me an' Howie at what you might call a critical moment. Howie knocked him out, and we didn't know what the hell to do with him. We still don't know how come he was tailing us."

He broke off, watching the man in the black as the latter thrust a gloved hand down into the slash pocket of his coat and brought out a pistol that was fitted with a silencer.

"Get rid of him."

Mo gaped. "Now?"

"No, tomorrow, after he's talked to a couple of hundred people!" the man in black snapped.

"But you mean right here? How'll I get him out of here?"

"That's your problem. You brought him in, and now you can get him out. Get this, Sipes. In this organization, each man will be given an opportunity to rectify his own errors. This is yours."

The man in black turned on his heel, left the room, and closed the door quietly.

Somewhere, a screen door slammed. Schoenling's heavy tread sounded on a stair. Lee Allyn counting the steps—one, two, three, four—and sat up, his back to the wall. Seven, eight, nine, ten, eleven, twelve. Twelve steps, then Schoenling was in the adjoining room with the Geiger counter.

Allyn swallowed past the dryness in his throat, and his pale, spectacled eyes took a quick tour of the room. To his left, a sagging cot, a soiled sheet crumpled at one end of it. Next to that an oak bureau with a crazed mirror hanging on the plastered wall.

In the wall directly opposite Allyn's present position was the open window—a second story window, which meant a drop of ten to a dozen feet, enough to break a leg or a neck. Next to that sat Mo Sipes with the silenced gun. The partitioning wall was unbroken except for the door into the adjoining room. There were sooty footprints on the matting where the man in black had stood, and the whole dingy rat-trap was illuminated by a single fly-blown bulb dangling from a center drop cord.

A metallic click brought Lee Allyn's gaze back to Mo Sipes. Mo was staring fixedly at the slight, pallid man on the floor, the silenced gun held low in his right hand, its safety off. Mo ran the tip of a red tongue along thin, dry lips.

"How you want to take it?" he asked in a husky whisper and took a step forward.

Allyn didn't answer. He was listening to what went on in the next room, to the muffled voice of "Reynox."

"...model has a neon flasher instead of 'phones or a microm-
eter."

The Geiger counter! The man in black was explaining the
instrument to Schoenling.

"I ast how you want to take it?" Mo Sipes repeated.

LEE ALLYN stood up. He took his time about it, his shoulder blades braced against the wall of a slowly reeling room. His
vision fogged. He pressed sweating palms against the wall until
the mist cleared. Then he was all right. Except for the pound-
ing of his heart and the cottony feeling inside his mouth, he
was all right.

He said steadily, "I'd like a cigarette."

"Sure." Mo Sipes put his left hand down into his pants pocket
and fingered out a limp cigarette. He stepped forward and
pushed the cigarette into Lee Allyn's lips. "Light?" Mo asked,
almost kindly. Keeping the silenced gun close to Allyn's middle,
Sipes brought out a cigarette lighter.

From the next room. Allyn caught some words. "...gamma
rays from any source enter the tube, they are attracted to the
central positive electrode...."

The lighter sparked, and Mo Sipes suddenly thrust the
flaming wick into Allyn's face. Allyn's head snapped instinctively back to slam against the wall. His indrawn breath had
sucked flame into his nose. His nostrils stung and smarting tears
momentarily blinded him.

Mo Sipes laughed. "You ain't going to be so nosy from here
on out, are you?"

Allyn tipped his head far to the right and the flame of the

lighter followed relentlessly. He blew down into the wick, and the flame went out.

"So I can light it again, smart guy," Mo Sipes said softly and thumbed the spark wheel. "See? Always works. You can go quick and easy, Mr. Nosy, and look natural at your funeral. Or you can die slow and the undertaker'll have to fix you up a new nose. Which'll it be? You gonna tell me how come you got interested all of a sudden in where Jake Katz was last night?"

The cold cigarette fell from Allyn's quivering lips.

The lighter backed off a few inches.

Allyn said, "I don't give a damn about Jake Katz. He's dead."

The close-set eyes narrowed slightly. "Who put you wise?"

From the next room: "... switch controls a potential of eight hundred volts...."

Allyn said hastily, "Captain Zero."

"Oh." Mo Sipes grinned in obvious disbelief. "So you got connections."

"Good ones," Allyn insisted. "Zero is a personal friend of mine. He's been in on this from the beginning. He's on to you and Schoenling, and your big boss knows it. Otherwise, why the sudden interest in Geiger counters? Figure it out for yourself. Mo. What kind of a chance have you got against a man like that? Why, he could be in this building right now, even in this room."

THE MAN IN BLACK was saying. "I'll turn on the switch, and we'll see how it works."

Allyn said. "You heard that, didn't you? You think the Geiger counter will register the presence of Captain Zero?"

Mo's snort of derision lacked conviction. "What do you think, yourself, Mr. Nosy?"

"I don't have to think." Allyn forced his lips into a cryptic smile as his gaze left Sipes' face and reached a remote quarter of the room. "No, I don't have to think. That neon indicator will light up like Times Square on New Year's Eve."

Sipes backed off uneasily, glanced out of the corner of his eye toward the spot which seemed to hold Lee Allyn's attention: Allyn took a shallow breath. One last bluff, he thought. Nothing to lose but a life. Everything to win. One good try.

He said mockingly, "You're not looking for Zero, are you, Mo?"

There was a harsh startled oath from the adjoining room. "Look at that lamp flash. My God, Schoenling!"

Sipes' gun veered toward the connecting door. Allyn sprang. His right hand caught Mo Sipes' forearm, deflecting the gun. His left reached up and out, got the dangling light bulb and hurled away in any direction.

Limited in its movements by the drop-cord, the light bulb described a blazing arc that ended in a sharp explosion as the globe smashed against the ceiling. Only a man who had spent half his life in blindness could move as swiftly and unerringly in sudden, total dark as Lee Allyn did now.

He heard the *plop* of the silenced gun and laughed. He got to the window. He was astride the sill, crouched low, fingers of both hands gripping the sill. Then the connecting door burst open. There was a wedge of light across the dark, and Allyn swung all the way over and let go.

He must have dropped two feet to the slanting shed roof that nobody had bothered to tell him about, landing on his right hip and shoulder. Then he was gone. Nothing could have stopped him—neither burst of gun fire from the open window nor any act of his own volition.

He was a tumbling avalanche of arms and legs, a difficult target that vanished over the eaves, that kept turning in mid-air, that finally hit the ground and sprawled face down. He came up onto his knees, onto the balls of his feet. He was running, his breath coming in strangled gasps.

And the dark closed about him like a cloak.

CHAPTER 9
ZERO HOUR

CHIEF-OF-POLICE ED CAVANAUGH turned from the intercom box through which he had been speaking to the radio dispatcher and stared at the soiled and battered man who sat on the straight chair opposite him.

"Hadn't you better see a doctor, Lee?"

"Oh, sure!" Lee Allyn said acidly. "I could see a doctor, all right, but in a matter of ten minutes from now, do you think he'd be able to see me?" He hooked an ankle over a knee and removed a rayon sock.

"I'll tell you what's wrong with me mostly. I'm scared. Suppose my bluff didn't get across. I tried to give Mo Sipes the idea that Lee Allyn was rescued by Captain Zero. Tried to take advantage of what I knew would happen to that Geiger counter in the next room. But just suppose Sipes, Schoenling and the rest conclude that Lee Allyn *is* Captain Zero."

He shook his head worriedly. "The snowball in hell would be fairly permanent by comparison to me."

Cavanaugh watched while Allyn discarded the rayon socks to replace them with heavy woolen ones that were equipped with rawhide soles.

"You mean you're going to vanish right here?"

"Where else? Is there a law against it?" Lee Allyn stood and began to remove his outer garments. "I'd like to vanish and stay vanished until I find out whether I'm over the deep end or not. But can I do that? I can, like hell! I have no more control over it than I have over the position of the sun. It's an affliction—not an asset."

"I wouldn't say that," Cavanaugh argued. "Except that your invisible prototype had thrown the fear of God into those killers, you wouldn't have got the break you needed. You'd be in some convenient drainage ditch right now. That Mo Sipes is a killer."

Allyn shivered in spite of the heat within the office. "Geiger counters!" he said. "If that idiot of a Wayland Pagget had kept his gadget out of this caper, we might have Sipes where we want him right now. Sipes and Schoenling and the big wheel."

"Did I tell you Pagget is related to one of the members of the Bachelors' Club?" Cavanaugh asked.

"Huh uh." Allyn was putting his horn-rimmed glasses into the pocket of his discarded trousers and, with the same movement, he brought out the plastic tube that contained his contact lenses.

"Pagget is Walter Bedlows' nephew," Cavanaugh said. "They're not on good terms, either. It seems Bedlows lost his fortune in a business venture which Pagget's father promoted."

He lit a cigarette. "It's just a little item we ran into when we were exploring every possible motive that might stem from the five hundred thousand dollar kitty."

"What do you think of the theory that the club members themselves have advanced?" Allyn asked as he began fitting the contact lenses beneath his eyelids.

"You mean, that some one member is trying to wipe out the rest in order to collect the total?" Cavanaugh shook his head. "Fantastic. That's why we got off on collateral relatives and ran across Pagget. We thought a collateral might try it where a member wouldn't dare, for the simple reason that the last man on his feet would be the killer and couldn't possibly collect the five hundred grand."

THE POLICE CHIEF became silent, watching in fascination as the flesh of Lee Allyn's face was gradually reduced to gray transparency while the bones of the skull were still clearly "defined.

"If that isn't the damnedest thing I ever saw!"

"*Yes?*" The shadowy skull that had been Lee Allyn's face was of course incapable of expression, but the tone of his voice clearly indicated his annoyance. "*I'm not putting on a sideshow act for your benefit, Ed.*"

Cavanaugh blew smoke toward the ceiling. "Hell, you're touchy tonight."

"*Maybe I am. I feel like the guy who was trapped in the maze*" with the monster. I've got to get the monster before he gets me, and I'm constantly running up dead-end passages and discovering that the one I'm chasing is directly behind me. It's not a situation conducive to a sunny disposition. What have you got, Ed, so far? Anything that I've missed?"

"Damned little. The slug they took out of poor Beckridge matched the one that killed Duncan Moore. According to witnesses at the bank stick-up, the gun was equipped with a silencer—" Cavanaugh broke off to stare uneasily at what remained of Lee Allyn—a wool T-shirt that was armless and headless, a pair of shorts that remained upright without any visible legs connecting them with the white socks.

And even as he watched, the rays emanating from Allyn's invisible body began to penetrate the scanty garments. Allyn was saying, *"I've seen the silenced gun—the business end of it. It belongs to Reynox."*

"To whom?" Cavanaugh scowled.

"Whatever his name is. Don't pay any attention to me, Ed. I'm tired and sore. My head aches, and I'm not sure that it's working properly. I've been associating that name Reynox with the lad who dolls himself up in a black hood. It just occurred to me that was the word that was on a stock certificate that slid out of a sack on the floor of the getaway car."

"Reynox," Cavanaugh mused. "Like the Reynox Company, you mean? I never heard of it."

"Neither have I." Zero moved over to Cavanaugh's desk and sat on a corner of it. He felt tired, sick, and discouraged. He would have given a good deal, just then, to be able to curl up

in a corner where no one would fall over him and go to sleep. Except that he wouldn't sleep. Fear and destiny had conspired to make an earthbound ghost of him, wearily haunting the night.

"Try and make a pattern out of it, Ed," he said. *"Just give it a whirl."*

Cavanaugh grunted. "You think I haven't?"

"We've got a gang of thieves who specialize in stolen securities. We've got McAlister and Moffet, both robbed and subsequently murdered. Next comes Duncan Moore, also murdered, but his safety deposit box is looted after Moore is dead—the day after.

"And not in a single instance was murder essential to the theft of these securities. The obvious motive for murder is this five hundred grand in survivorship insurance, which doesn't fit in at all with Schoenling and stolen securities. Nothing fits. It's the damnedest mess I've ever run into."

CAVANAUGH TIPPED back in his chair and stared at the two pin-pricks of reflected light which represented the contact lenses on the eyes of his invisible guest. Cavanaugh smiled slightly.

"You make it tough," he said quietly.

"Okay. So you go ahead and make it easy."

"I can't do that, but I think I can boil it down. The crimes are all connected—will you grant that?"

"Sure."

"So there has to be a connecting factor. Let's not worry now about what it is, let's just call it X."

Zero groaned. *"And I flunked algebra."*

"X," Cavanaugh went on, "is something that each of the three men had that somebody else wanted. McAlister's safe is blown and he's robbed of X, among other things. Shortly afterward, McAlister commits suicide which turns out to murder. Then Moffet's safe is ripped open, he is robbed of X, among other things, and shortly after he dies of a heart attack that turns out to be murder. Next, Duncan Moore is murdered—a straightforward job of killing, this time—and the following day Moore's safety deposit box is looted. Did the safety deposit box contain X?"

"We don't know what it contained," Zero said.

"That's it. And that establishes our motive, to my backward way of reasoning," Cavanaugh said. "The three murders look like a feverish and extremely successful attempt on the part of somebody to keep the exact nature of X a secret. I don't say that the motive of gain isn't wrapped up in it. But fear is the strongest emotion, and I think fear of the discovery of X is what is behind the deaths of these three old men. And it must be *some* secret to kill three men."

Zero remained thoughtfully silent for a moment. Then, *"That makes some order of chaos. I'm beginning to feel not quite so thoroughly licked."*

Cavanaugh dropped his cigarette into an ash tray, leaned forward, his forearms resting on the desk.

"Lee, that bank stick-up was too perfectly timed. Somebody knew that Cline and Beckridge and the federal tax man were going to open Moore's box. Cline is administrator for the Moore estate and made all the arrangements. It looks like a leak in the

Earhart-Cline office. It looks," he added significantly, "like our friend Bardon."

"Or the office boy," Zero injected for the sake of argument.

Cavanaugh frowned, shook his head. "We've gone into Bardon's background pretty carefully without finding a blemish. He's a local boy, the son of a Jessop Street tailor. He made a good war record, both in combat and later, Stateside, in the Army Finance Department. Cline speaks highly of him. All that on the credit side. The fact remains that Bardon has handled securities for all three of the men who have been murdered."

"The same could be said of Cline," Zero argued. *"Or Earhart. And I could drag out the names of a hundred people who have dealt with that firm and are alive and kicking today. And there's another little item you've overlooked—Bardon's alibi."*

And, Zero might have added, Cavanaugh didn't know how iron-clad that alibi actually was. After all, Bardon couldn't have killed two different men at the same time on opposite sides of the city.

"Maybe I'm just prejudiced because he's got an alibi," Cavanaugh admitted. He smiled thinly. "Too many years on the police force can warp a man's viewpoint. Have you seen Bardon's girl—the one he intends to marry?"

"No," Zero replied. *"Who is she?"*

"Girl by the name of Ann Gerard. She's a model at Yoder's Department Store, according to that Miss Franzer who lives in the apartment below the late Duncan Moore. Miss Franzer is with the same firm, incidentally, and she quite obviously doesn't think much of Ann Gerard. She lived with Miss Franzer for a time, there at the Hildebrand."

"Maybe Miss Franzer is jealous," Zero suggested.

"Maybe. Ann Gerard has a good deal that Miss Franzer might be envious of. Gerard is the kind of a woman a man would cut his throat for."

"Like that, huh?" Zero laughed softly. *"I'll have to look in on this lady. But you mentioned that Cline is the executor of the Moore estate. Who benefits by Moore's will?"*

"CHARITIES, MOSTLY, except for a ten thousand dollar bequest to his friend Walter Bedlows, who happens to be the only member of the Bachelors' Club who is in rather desperate financial straights."

"And you say Wayland Pagget is Bedlows' nephew?" Zero mused. *"Suppose Bedlows were to be the last of the bachelors to remain alive. That would mean five hundred and ten thousand dollars, wouldn't it? And if Bedlows died intestate—"*

"He won't," Cavanaugh interrupted. "I told you Bedlows hates his nephew. He's had an iron-clad will drawn up that leaves Pagget out in the cold."

"You mean," Zero said slowly, *"that a man who is in desperate financial straights, as you put it, draws up a will to keep his nephew out in the cold? That's like a tourniquet to keep the turnip from bleeding, isn't it?"*

Cavanaugh stirred uncomfortably in his chair. This was evidently something he had not considered. "Well," he said, "there's always the possibility, I suppose, that Bedlows *might* be the winner of that five hundred grand. He's got the same stake the rest of the members have and, as far as anybody knows, the same chance of winning. But—"he shrugged—"could be you've got an angle there."

"Could be." Zero reached across the desk and drew the telephone toward himself. *"Mind if I use this?"*

Cavanaugh shook his head and watched the handset float up from the desk to remain poised two feet above the glass surface. He heard the running click of the dial, cursed softly, and swiveled around so that he wouldn't have to witness the phenomenon of an invisible man using a telephone.

Zero said, *"Cheer up, Ed. Don't be surprised if I have those stolen securities for you within a few hours."*

"That'll help. But I'd rather have that damned killer."

"Don't ask Santa Claus for too much," Zero said whimsically. *"There are other little boys and girls, you know."* One in particular named Ned Bardon, he thought, who was in a tight jam and who didn't seem to be at home at the moment. He put the handset down.

"I was trying to get Bardon," he said. *"Wonder if he's out somewhere with that glorious girl friend of his? You might give me a lift to Ann Gerard's place, Ed. I don't have a whole lot of luck hailing taxi cabs."*

Cavanaugh grunted and stood up. He indicated Lee Allyn's discarded outer clothing. "What about that stuff?"

"You might drop that off at my lodging," Zero said as he slid off the desk. *"There's a box at the corner of the garage that my landlady uses for old newspapers. You could stash my clothes in there."*

Obviously displeased with his rôle of valet and chauffeur to an invisible man, Cavanaugh jerked up the clothing and made a wad of it. At the door he paused, his eyes scouting the apparently empty room in an effort to locate Zero.

"There's one more thing," he growled. "Last night in Moore's apartment, what was the idea of sampling the champagne?"

"I wanted to find out if it was as flat as it looked," Zero answered honestly.

"It was," Cavanaugh said. "It naturally would be, open that length of time. But did you ever see so much flat champagne in your life?"

"Meaning why didn't Bardon and Moore drink it before it went flat?"

"That's it."

"I've been wondering about that," Zero said. There was probably a simple and perfectly logical explanation for the flat champagne. He'd have to ask Bardon about that. He'd have to ask Bardon about quite a number of things.

MISS ADA FRANZER, adhering strictly to schedule, was in bed by half-past-midnight. She always raced Basil-the-clock with her bedtime preparations, and invariably she would hear the single chime just before she dozed off. She would think smugly, Poor Basil—Basil-the-man, of course—and so drift off into an untroubled sleep.

But not tonight. It was, she told herself, the heat. It was not—and she felt she must be quite firm with herself about this—the fact that roughly twenty-four hours ago she had stood back from her east window—her heart in her throat, the echoes of gunfire ringing in her ears—and had realized that murder had rudely jostled her in passing.

That, she resolved firmly, was an experience she must forget. It had nothing to do with the fact that darkness had a smothering quality which she felt particularly when her eyes were closed.

She opened her eyes. A pale night glow got in beneath the lowered awning outside the east window. There was a street lamp nearby and its rays touched the white marquisette curtains on either side of the casement. There was never enough light through this window to bother her; there was only enough to remind her that she was not buried alive.

Now she stared at the white blur of the curtains and saw an oddly shaped shadow projected against one of them—a slim vertical line extending from the valance of the awning to within a few inches of the sill and ending in a loop.

"Like the outline of a spoon," she whispered only because the shadow was very much more like that of a noose. When it remained persistently nooselike, Miss Franzer got out of bed and went to the window. There she knelt, parting the curtains, and tried to see the object that had cast such a shadow.

Whatever it was, it was either too minute or the light was too uncertain for her to see it. Yet when she let the curtain fall again, the shadow returned. A noose.

An omen? Miss Franzer wondered. Omens had never seemed to her to be very practical. Surely if this was one, its impracticability was clearly demonstrated.

"Because why bother me with it?" Miss Franzer asked. "The

person who ought to be seeing a noose in front of his eyes is the person who killed Mr. Moore."

A person, Miss Franzer remembered suddenly, who was still at large.

CHAPTER 10
HOT BONDS

ANN GERARD stood at the wide window of her apartment living room overlooking Outer Drive. The dusky midnight skyline of old Pendleville was pricked here and there by a lighted window, and above, less sparsely scattered, there were stars.

Ned Bardon stood beside her. She caught his hand without looking at him, something frantic in her manner as though, beyond the darkness into which she stared, she had sighted something terrifying.

"Take it easy," Ned Bardon said gently.

She looked at him then. Some of the tautness went out of her face. Her smile was fleeting.

"How long have you been this way?" he asked soberly.

"What way, darling?"

"Jumpy."

"Since lunch," she said. "Since you told me about Captain Zero and the fat Schoenling and all." She tipped her head to the right to rest it for a moment against his shoulder. Ned Bardon put up his right hand and stroked her shimmering hair.

She said, "And you know they suspect you of killing Duncan Moore."

"They maybe did," he admitted. "But nobody can be in two places at once. Cavanaugh knows perfectly well where I was at midnight last night—miles away from the Hildebrand apartments."

"But there's Schoenling," she said. "Darling, how can you play both ends against the middle that way?"

His hand dropped in a kind of hopeless gesture. "Is there any other way? Schoenling has got me and he knows it. My only hope of breaking that frame he's wrapped around me is Captain Zero. We'll muddle through some way, I feel."

He broke off as an electric buzzer sounded. Ann was suddenly erect, her every fiber tense, her wonderful eyes—they were violet with flecks of gold in them—on his face.

"What—?" Her coral lips shaped the word she scarcely whispered.

"The door buzzer, I presume," he said calmly.

"But who? At this hour?"

"There's a way to find out." He released her hand, started toward the vestibule, but Ann caught his arm.

"I'll go," she insisted.

He looked at her. Now she was all right, her lovely face composed, nerves under control.

"Right," he said. He watched her move across the room, the pale green gown she wore clinging sweetly to the curve of her hips and falling away in frosty folds to the jade green carpet on the floor. Green was for Ann, to compliment her glorious red hair.

"Yes?" she was saying into the speaking tube. "But who is it, please?" Then, "Ned—" anxiously.

He went on to the vestibule. Ann had a hand over the mouthpiece of the speaking tube. Her eyes were wide and bright with danger.

"Some man. He wants to know if you're here. He wouldn't give me his name."

"Right." The muscles at the corners of Ned Bardon's mouth were tight. He reached out, gently took her hand away from the tube. Her hand was cold, in spite of the summer night, and he held it while he spoke. "This is Ned Bardon."

"Zero, Bardon," came from the tube.

Ann Gerard's indrawn breath was audible.

"Yes?" Bardon said guardedly.

"I know this is on intrusion, but I'd like to come up. That is, if it won't be too much of a strain on Miss Gerard's nerves."

"On the contrary, I think she'll enjoy the experience," Bardon said. He thumbed the button that operated the magnetic lock on the door downstairs. He looked at the girl. Her eyes still fixed upon his face, she shook her head slowly back and forth.

"I'll never be able to go through with it, Ned."

"Yes you will."

"I've never had hysterics before, but I think now I'll have them. Yes, I will, Ned. This above all. This invisible man—invisible *detective*. Cavanaugh was enough. Now this—this—" She started to laugh, and Bardon caught her shoulders roughly.

123

"Stop it, Ann." He was shaking her, his lower lip nipped in his teeth. "I'd rather cut off my right arm than to slap you, but so help me, Ann—"

SHE STOPPED laughing. "But, Ned. How? What?"

"Just treat him like anybody else."

"That's not possible—somebody you can't see?" Laughter choked her for a moment. She fought it back. "Anybody but Zero, Ned. Your fat Schoenling. A gangster—anybody but a—a nothingness. A ghost."

"Ghosts wear sheets." Bardon forced a laugh. He still held her shoulders, and now he turned her about and gave her a gentle push toward the living room. "Go in and sit down. Look, honey, it's no different than if you were blind. Think of it that way, and remember what you're like—what a beautiful woman you are. He's on our side. We've got everything to gain by cooperating with him."

She moved slowly across the living room, paused, her back toward Ned. For an instant she was tempted to dash into her bedroom, to lock herself in. Just to get away from it all.

But she kept on to the stiff little French enameled chair, sat down, ankles crossed, bosom high and proud, her hands quiet in her lap. Only the shallowness of her breathing betrayed her nervousness.

"Fine," Ned Bardon said. He lighted a cigarette, there in the vestibule. His hands were steady, his face waxy in the flame. He snapped the lighter shut, flashed her a smile wreathed in smoke, and turned as a knock came at the door.

Ann Gerard momentarily closed her eyes. Now, she thought.

After this I can do anything. Anything at all.

"Good evening, Bardon."

Ann's eyelids opened. The voice was any man's voice, calm, pleasant, yet oddly compelling. Bardon had opened the door wide enough to admit an elephant, and now he stood with his hand out as though grasping something tangible. Ann watched Ned's hand go up and down, finally sweep away in a gesture of welcome.

"Come in, Captain. I'd like you to meet my fiancée," Bardon was saying.

But, darling, Ann thought, he's already in! And she stared wide-eyed at footprints in the thick pile of the carpet—footprints that alternately formed and dissolved as they progressed straight toward her chair.

The Man in Black

"Ann, dear—" Bardon began.

"You're not going to scream now, are you, Miss Gerard?"

That was Zero's voice. The footprints were directly between her and Ned Bardon. She looked up, her lips apart. She saw only Ned, his smile fixed. It struck her then that she must be looking *straight through* Captain Zero.

"I—I think I am," Ann stammered. She raised her hand limply and it was immediately caught in warmth and pressure. She closed her eyes, and it was any man's hand, alive and strong. Then her own hand was released and she heard quiet, gentle laughter.

"You can't imagine what a treat this is for me," Zero was saying. *"You didn't scream and you're not going to. Bardon, you're a lucky man. Miss Gerard has an excellent nervous system."*

Ann opened her eyes. Ned Bardon was pulling up a chair.

"No, never mind," Zero was saying. *"I've already found a spot, thank you."*

AND SO he had. Ann saw one end of the cushion of the love-seat was depressed beneath Zero's invisible weight. Bardon shrugged easily and sat down in the chair he had intended for Captain Zero.

"There's a question," said the calm voice from the direction of the love-seat. *"About that champagne in Moore's apartment last night."*

Ned Bardon nodded. "I wondered how soon somebody was going to start worrying about that."

"Why didn't you and Moore drink it?"

"There was something wrong with it," Ned Bardon explained. "I think it was spoiled. No bubbles."

"It was flat when you opened it, then?"

"Right." Ned Bardon glanced over at Ann to see how she was doing. She was all right, a little pale beneath her rouge, perhaps, but otherwise, she was perfectly composed and perfectly beautiful. He smiled at her.

"There's another item."

Ned Bardon turned to the love-seat. "Yes?"

"And I was wondering if we oughtn't to step into the next room. After all, it doesn't concern Miss Gerard."

Bardon was shaking his head. "I'm afraid it does, Captain. Ann and I have made a little pact. No secrets. Neither now nor after we're married. So if your question concerns Schoenling, the man I inadvertently killed in Jessop Street, the mysterious girl who ran away—anything at all—feel perfectly free to speak right here."

"You see, Captain," Ann said evenly, "Ned has told me everything."

"Very well then, Bardon. This concerns Schoenling. Have you seen him today?"

Ned Bardon tapped cigarette ashes into a tray that rested on the mahogany end table. He nodded. "Twice. He had the brass to come into my office around noon. I stalled him off, told him I'd go into the deal with him only if I was accepted as a full partner. He said there was somebody else he'd have to consult."

"The big wheel," Zero commented. *"Go on."*

"And again tonight. He brought me some securities which I'm supposed to turn over for the best price I can get. He told me definitely that I was in. I'd get a split on the net profit, he said."

"*Schoenling is a diplomat,*" Zero said dryly. "*Anything to keep you happy. I can assure you that you're not in. You see, I had a run-in with the big wheel myself.*"

"You did?" Ann gasped.

"*Yes. He's quite a character. Dolls himself up in a black hood so that his own mother wouldn't know him. You see, I have a friend by the name of Allyn on the World. Lee Allyn. I asked him to investigate the late Jake Katz for me.*"

"And did he get anywhere with it?" Bardon asked eagerly.

"*He got himself in a nice jam,*" Zero said and laughed quietly. "*The Jessop Street mob that Katz used to run with, pulled off a job at the Inland Street branch bank. Allyn was taken along for the ride. It would have been a one-way trip except that I managed to trail them to a temporary hideout and lend Allyn a hand.*"

"But did he find out anything about this woman Ned rescued last night?" Ann Gerard persisted.

"*He picked up very little information of any sort,*" Zero told them. "*Too busy trying to stay alive. But he did overhear a conversation between Schoenling and this masked wonder which concerns you, Bardon. They're going to increase the pressure to keep you in line.*"

ANN GERARD'S indrawn breath was audible and tremulous. Her lovely eyes were fixed on Bardon. "Darling, isn't there any way out? Any way at all?"

Bardon didn't answer, merely indicated the love-seat where Zero was with a jerk of his hand.

"*I'm afraid,*" Zero said, "*that you'll have to stick with it, Bardon, until we can get a line on this mystery woman. And that may come a whole lot sooner than we expect. Right now everything seems to be* coming their way. But the current is bound to change. Now, about these stolen securities you're supposed to turn over for the mob—where are they now?"

Bardon said, "I've got them in my car." He laughed nervously. "If I had to get rid of them, I'm not at all sure I'd know how to go about it."

"You'll get rid of them," Zero said. "Suppose you let me see them. Right now."

"Right." Bardon stood, took a final drag from his cigarette, went into the vestibule. As he left the apartment he released the night latch on the door.

Ann Gerard pushed her coral lips into a smile as she addressed the unseen presence on the love-seat. "I was about to make high-balls when you arrived, Captain. Shall I?"

"By all means," Zero said, "for yourself and Bardon. None for me, thanks."

"If you'll excuse me?"

"Certainly."

Zero watched Ann get up and move gracefully into the dining-L of the big room and thence to the kitchen door. She looked back, the curling ends of her glorious red hair brushing a shoulder.

"There are cigarettes on the coffee table, Captain."

"No thanks," Zero said. "I'll just enjoy my surroundings. These are nice etchings on this wall here. Particularly the Rheims cathedral."

"Relics of my art class days."

"Souvenirs, perhaps. Hardly relics. Your own work?"

"With quite a bit of help from my instructors."

Ann Gerard moved out of Zero's range of vision, but left the door into the kitchen open. Zero stood and sauntered about the tastefully furnished room.

Ann Gerard worried him, he didn't know why. Perhaps it was only because she had worried Cavanaugh and in some manner had excited the chief's suspicion. She must have been wholly conscious of her beauty yet she had no inclination to use it. She was pleasant, unassuming, and refined. Just a nice girl, and it was perhaps this quality that had, to Cavanaugh's jaundiced eyes, seemed incompatible with her physical attraction.

Zero paused beside a mahogany knee-hole desk and coolly flipped through the pages of an address book. Aside from Bardon's name, there was only one other that was familiar—that of Miss Ada Franzer of the Hildebrand apartments. Cavanaugh had said that Ann Gerard had formerly shared Miss Franzer's quarters.

Zero crouched over the wastebasket beside the desk. It contained a number of advertising circulars, an empty tube that had once held household cement, some odd scraps of felt. He brought out the scraps and spread them across an invisible knee—a torn circular piece of gray about nine inches in diameter, a square piece of green from which a circle the exact size of the torn one had been cut.

Zero was rolling the scraps into a ball when Ann Gerard entered with tray and glasses. She paused, her eyes wide. And then her lips curved into a charming smile.

"You can't imagine how odd that looks, Captain—those

scraps wadding themselves up as though they'd suddenly come alive!"

"I'm afraid I'm guilty of the unpardonable crime of snooping," Zero said easily as he dropped the felt scraps into the basket. ANN GERARD put the tray down on the coffee table and sank onto the cushions of the sofa. Her eyes found his footprints on the soft carpet and then lifted to a flattering height where she assumed his face to be.

"And I suppose you find me disappointingly ordinary person."

"On the contrary." Was that the right reply? Zero found himself momentarily disconcerted. His eyes left the lovely face and gave its setting a quick compassing glance. Maybe it was right here—the thing that had worried Cavanaugh.

The room seemed divorced of personality, like a show window of a furniture store. But there were other such rooms, thousands of them, and you viewed them from the streets through picture windows, show-cases of prosperity maintained by families that did their living in kitchens and rumpus rooms less open to the public inspection.

Ann Gerard was saying, "I put a new felt pad on the base of this lamp—" with a wave of her hand—"as you undoubtedly deduced from the clues left carelessly behind for the moths to take care of."

"And the detectives," he said, laughing.

"Are you sure you won't have a drink, Captain?"

"No thanks."

She tonged an ice cube into a glass, frowning slightly. "Do

131

you think you'll be able to do something for Ned? To get him out of this horrible mess?"

"Of course."

She closed her eyes briefly and when she opened them they were shiny with tears. "Because I love him more than I ever supposed I could love anyone."

The door opened and Ned Bardon came into the vestibule with a briefcase in his hand.

"Don't tell him I said so," Ann Gerard said, her sober gaze on the tall young man as he carried the briefcase to the desk.

"Don't tell him what?" Ned Bardon asked. He looked at Ann.

"Secrets, darling."

"A fine thing!" Ned Bardon zipped open the briefcase and turned it upside down to shake two thick paper-wrapped packages onto the desk. "There you are." Trying to see on all sides of himself at once, he added, "Or are you?"

Zero was standing on Bardon's left. *"I don't carry a knife. Would you mind opening them?"*

Bardon produced a gold penknife, cut the strings on the two packages, then walked to the sofa and sat down beside Ann. He sat well forward on the cushions, elbows on knees, his hands clasped in front of him.

He didn't take his eyes off the desk as the brown paper was flattened and the thick sheaf of securities floated up from it to fan out like a hand of bridge cards. Ned Bardon shivered slightly.

"You could make a fortune on the stage, Captain," he said.

Zero squared the stack of securities without replying, opened the second bundle and examined them in a similar manner.

"Darling, your drink's getting warm," Ann said.

"There's no Reynox stock here, Bardon."

"Well, hardly!" Bardon picked up his glass and tasted the drink. "You weren't expecting any, were you?"

"I was," Zero said. He turned from the desk, came to the sofa, and stood facing the couple. *"I have reason to believe that Duncan Moore's safety deposit box contained some Reynox stock."*

Bardon's eyes caught the glinting pinpoints of reflected light from Zero's contact lenses. Bardon shook his head slightly. He smiled.

"I don't know the source of your information, of course, Captain, but I'd be inclined to question its accuracy. To my knowledge there's never been an offering of Reynox stock. Every share is held by members of the Reynolds and Oxford families.

"The firm started small and grew big. They've cleaned up a mint of money for themselves in pharmaceuticals, and I imagine any one of them would prefer to part with his or her right arm than a share of Reynox."

"Darling," Ann put in, "didn't you tell me that one of the Reynoldses disappeared in darkest Africa or somewhere last year?"

NED BARDON drew a short impatient gesture. "That's beside the point. Anyway, it was an Oxford and he disappeared in some South American jungle. There was quite a stir about it in the papers at the time. He's never been heard from since."

"Suppose he was kidnaped by Indians or pirates or some thing," Ann suggested.

Ned Bardon laughed. "Oh, sure. Or even by poor old Duncan Moore."

"Wait a minute," Zero said. *"I'm beginning to like Miss Gerard's ideas better than yours, Bardon."*

"I always have," Ned Bardon said, "up to now. If you're thinking that stock belonging to Roy Oxford has filtered back into circulation from South America, you're both letting your imaginations get away from you. Anything like that would create a minor tempest in the financial world."

"What I meant," Zero interrupted, *"is that Miss Gerard has perhaps inadvertently suggested a new angle on the old Spanish prisoner con game. The whole set-up has a hammy flavor that suckers go for. Suppose it were to be nosed around in the right places that this Roy Oxford was being held for ransom in a remote quarter of the globe by a group of bandits or political outcasts, and that all he had with which to raise the ransom were these stock certificates. I know,"* Zero said hastily as Bardon started to laugh, *"I said it was hammy."*

"How hammy can you get!"

"Any con man will tell you it takes ham and brass," Zero insisted. *"The Spanish prison game has been worked hundreds of times simply because the situation captures the imagination. This has an element of fact. The sucker remembers reading that Roy Oxford vanished into the South American jungle. Think about it a moment, Bardon. Did Duncan Moore ever mention Reynox stock to you?"*

"Never. He—" Bardon broke off. He looked at Ann and his expression was a trifle foolish. "Wait a minute. Maybe I'm getting a little ahead of myself, Captain."

"Then Mr. Moore did mention it?" Ann asked.

"Not to me," Bardon replied. "But this noon when I was in Cline's office, Cline asked me if Duncan Moore had any Reynox stock, because a while back Moore had 'phoned him and asked some rather discreet question about Reynox.

"Both Cline and I agreed that Moore couldn't possibly have any Reynox stock. And that still goes, Captain, though I withdraw my objection to the hammy con game. It just might work, with forged certificates and the proper promotion."

"I think it has worked," Zero said dryly. *"I think it's worked very well. I believe we've at last found X."*

"X?" Ann Gerard and Ned Bardon spoke in unison.

"Something Cavanaugh and I were talking about," Zero said. He turned, went back to the desk and once more squared up the two packets of stolen securities. *"Wrap these up, will you, Bardon. Address them to Chief-of-Police Cavanaugh, and see that they get into the mail at once."*

Bardon polished off his drink and stood. He would have gone to the desk except that Ann caught him by the sleeve of his suit coat. He looked down at her and her eyes were shiny with alarm.

"What's wrong with it?" Bardon wanted to know.

"Schoenling," she whispered. "The fat man. That's what's wrong, darling."

Bardon made sounds like laughter. "Good lord, you didn't think I was actually going to peddle them, did you? Look, darling, I'll stall Schoenling. He knows you can't turn over any securities, even those acquired through legitimate channels, over night. It takes time."

Ann was shaking her lovely head. "Suppose it gets out? The newspapers—there could be a leak somewhere. They'd kill you, darling."

Zero said, *"Bardon doesn't have to put his name and return address on the packages."*

"But the police," Ann objected. "They have ways of finding out things. Perhaps they'd know from Ned's handwriting."

"So what?" Ned Bardon cut in. "I'm not ashamed of returning stolen property, especially inasmuch as I didn't steal it."

"And I still like Miss Gerard's ideas better than yours," Zero said. *"She's thinking of the woman angle, of course. The mystery woman in Jessop Street last night, Bardon. That's one thing we've got to be damned sure about before we upset Schoenling. The fat man doesn't look like a good loser to me. If he's got the goods he says he's got, he can slap back with a murder indictment anytime he feels like it."*

Ned Bardon thoughtfully sucked a molar. "What the hell am I going to do with those securities then?"

Even before he had stopped speaking, he saw the answer taking shape. Captain Zero's invisible fingers were re-wrapping the two packages of securities. String tied itself into an intricate knot.

A pen sprang out of its standard and scrawled boldly across the paper covering. And in the upper left hand corner of the face of each package the pen wrote, by way of return address, "O."

"Now," Zero said, *"if you'll drop them into the mail box on your way home, Bardon. I'd do it, but two packages look so silly floating along in the air two or three feet above the sidewalk. And this gives*

you a way out in case Schoenling gets you around a dark corner. You can always say that Zero stole the loot from you."

"In case Schoenling gets you around a dark corner," Ann Gerard repeated, shivering.

CHAPTER 11
A VERY DARK CORNER

MO SIPES closed the door and leaned against it. The close-set eyes in his sharp, narrow face flicked about the dingy office behind Paul Schoenling's pawnshop and returned to the immense figure standing two yards back from the threshold. Fat Paul was dressed in his soiled white suit. His floppy Panama was on top of the desk litter.

"You going somewhere, Fat Paul?" Mo Sipes' hands were in his trouser pockets, and the pocket lining was pasty from sweat.

"Perhaps," Fat Paul replied coldly. "Perhaps not. Why did you come here? You were told to scatter, weren't you?"

"I scattered. Me and Howie." A shudder rippled across Mo Sipes' shoulders. "Howie's scattered right now—all over Canal Street."

Schoenling's eyebrows peaked. "Oh?" Softly.

"A cop got him."

"You were with him?"

"I was with him. Me and Howie. We're the ones. That nosy son must have went straight to the cops. Me and Howie was hotter'n little red firecrackers. I tried the bus depot, and it's crawling with coppers. Same for the rattlers."

"So you came here."

"So I came here," Mo Sipes said. He moved away from the door to the desk chair which he tipped up to dislodge a heap of old magazines that were piled on the seat of it. He sat down, his eyes still fixed on the fat man's face.

"Yellow?" Schoenling enquired mildly.

"Just cautious, Fat Paul." Mo Sipes took out a battered package of cigarettes and lighted one. "After all, I'm the guy that gunned the copper, ain't I? And me and Howie was hot, thanks to the damned nosy son."

"But why come here?" Schoenling inquired. He chuckled somewhat uneasily. "I can't possibly hang you on the wall like a pawned guitar. What do you expect me to do?"

"I want my split, Fat Paul. I want it so I can buy me a powder. I gotta get out of town, don't I? So I want my dough."

"I can let you have some money."

"Now," Mo Sipes said, and his mouth relaxed in a thin-lipped smile, "now you're makin' sense. About two Gs. I ought to get myself a powder for that."

Schoenling nodded agreeably. "You should indeed. You certainly should. Make yourself at home, Mo. I'll be right back." He turned, crossed the room to open a door at the foot of the stairs leading to his apartment above.

He closed the door after him, and Mo Sipes could hear Fat Paul's slow, heavy tread on the steps. Then an uneasy silence crowded into the building. Mo Sipes cleared his throat nervously to break it, but it put itself together and lay oppressively upon him.

He looked at his watch. 1:35. What was taking Fat Paul so long? Mo Sipes remembered the safe in the corner of the office. Why had Fat Paul gone upstairs to get the two G's?

And what—the thought formed itself from the crawling worms of fear in Mo Sipes' brain—what was to prevent Schoenling from double-crossing him? Fat Paul always managed to keep his own hands clean. Suppose Fat Paul decided it would be a good deal to go to the cops? They'd bargain with Schoenling, the lousy cops would, to get their hands on the man who had gunned Beckridge.

Mo Sipes' thin mouth twisted about. "I'll kill the fat slob," he muttered. He dropped his cigarette to the floor and toed it out with his first step toward the door at the foot of the stairway. He opened the door with his left hand, and his right pulled a stubby black automatic.

Something warm and sinewy whipped about his neck from behind. As it tightened, his lathlike body was bowed backwards. Rolling his eyes down, to right and left, he saw nothing beyond his own prominent cheekbones. His cry of panic remained a soundless lump in his throat. Something he couldn't see tangled his leg in an effort to trip him.

Mo Sipes reeled. He flung up his right arm, pointed the gun across his left shoulder, and jerked the trigger.

FAT PAUL heard the shot from downstairs. Schoenling's broad face fell open, and there was a sensation in the region of his stomach like that experienced during a fast drop in an elevator. Schoenling jerked the door open, went plunging down the stair to stop at the halfway point and crouch low.

From this post he could see into his office through the open door. He could see a pair of skinny legs wearing navy blue spread in a narrow V across the floor. And he could see a portion of his desk.

The papers that littered his desk were moving, not in a random manner that suggested a draft through an open window, but rather as though unseen hands were pawing through them.

Captain Zero. In Schoenling's office, Zero had killed Sipes. That was something Fat Paul would worry about only if he could conceive of some way to avoid being handled as Mo Sipes had been handled.

Schoenling pushed away from the door, reeled across the room, and fumbled open the door of the closet from which he took a small black box—his portable Geiger counter. He put it down on the table beside the bed and flipped the switch.

He stared at the bull's-eye glass that covered the tiny neon lamp and waited for the tube to warm. Presently, the bull's-eye flashed its eerie warning and went out. It came on again at once, then off. On. Off. On. Flashing rapidly, but by no means as rapidly as Schoenling's heart was beating.

Schoenling dipped into the table drawer and took out his little automatic pistol. He dropped this into the left hand pocket of his white suit coat—much good a gun would do when you couldn't see the target—picked up the Geiger counter, and hustled to the door. He thrust his big head out into the hall, listened to utter and forbidding silence.

He held the Geiger counter by its strap handle in his right hand and glanced down at the glass bull's-eye. Was the tiny neon lamp flashing at greater frequency, or was that merely his imagination? He didn't know, couldn't be sure about the thing at all. Damn all gadgets anyway!

He turned to the right, away from the back stairway, and tiptoed to the opposite end of the hall. The building was a remodeled version of an old residence, and there was a front stairway which communicated with the pawnshop on the first floor.

As Schoenling descended into the dark, he became convinced that the flashing of the Geiger counter was less frequent, which meant that with every step he was putting more space between himself and Captain Zero. Schoenling breathed easier.

He entered the pawnshop where a dim night light burned behind the bars of the cashier's cage at the rear. There, in the center of the barren floor, Schoenling crouched hugely, blew dust from an incised circle in one of the boards to reveal a pull-ring which he raised to its vertical position.

He stepped back from the edge of the basement trap door, took hold of the ring, and heaved upwards. The trap opened and the scant light was swallowed in the maw of the basement stairs.

Schoenling started down, tracking in the dust on the treads. He didn't turn on a light, for he didn't need one. Every niche and cranny of the old building was familiar to him. Now and then he would pause and watch the Geiger counter, and he was reminded of a game he had played as a child: one of his playmates would hide something and while little Paul Schoenling hunted for it, his giggling companion would say *colder* if Paul was getting farther away from the hidden object and *warmer* whenever Paul approached it.

The Geiger counter told him now that he was getting colder in relation to Captain Zero's present location, and this was gratifying indeed. Groping with his left hand, he located the side of the steam boiler. He put out a cautious foot and discovered heavy plank beneath. He drew the foot back and crouched in the darkness, resting the Geiger counter on the floor beside him in order to use both hands.

SCHOENLING'S FINGERS dug into a crack between two of the heavy planks, got the one nearest him up on edge. It was, he knew, about a yard in length—the approximate distance between the side of the boiler and the wall. A smell of dankness came up from the opening beneath.

He straightened carefully and sidled to the front of the boiler where he put the plank down on end. There were, he knew, three such planks, and they covered the yard square opening of an old cistern. A very deep cistern. A very wide cistern. Anyone who happened to fall into it would not get out again without assistance.

When he had removed the three planks and the watery trap yawned at its widest, Schoenling picked up the Geiger counter and climbed the skeleton stairs.

Schoenling put the Geiger counter down on the glass top of a counter that contained photographic supplies. He then removed his suit coat which he dropped over the Geiger counter in such a manner that he could scoop it up again, in passing, and take the counter with him without exciting too much suspicion, especially in the dim illumination afforded by the night lamp back of the cashier's cage.

Now, in shirt sleeves, Schoenling turned toward the back of the shop, locating the connecting door beyond the tall wardrobe case containing clothing which he had accepted as security on loans. On the other side of that was his office, the dead body of Mo Sipes, and the invisible Captain Zero.

Schoenling took a deep breath and headed for that door. Mo Sipes lay on the floor, on his back. Oddly, he had his automatic clutched in his right hand. It might have been suicide except that the bullet hole was in Mo's left temple, indicating clearly that there had been a struggle, that Mo had attempted to use his gun, and that, in the last possible instant, somebody had managed to turn the muzzle against Mo's head.

Tiny eyes scouted the office for some indication of his audience. There was none. The papers on his desk were somewhat more tidy than they had been, but there was neither sound nor movement to indicate the presence of Captain Zero.

Schoenling's eyes went back to the late Mr. Sipes where he lay on the floor.

"Got to get out of here," Schoenling gasped. "Right now. Got to get out. Take the loot, of course."

Oh, certainly, take the loot, he thought. Do you follow me, Captain Zero? You do, I'm sure. Quite literally.

If there was an expression of panic on Schoenling's face as he turned in the door, it was genuine. It could not help but convince the unseen pair of eyes that watched. Schoenling stumbled back across the pawnshop, threw a single terrified glance over a huge shoulder, caught up his coat and the partially concealed Geiger counter at the same time.

As he moved to the open trap above the basement stairs, Schoenling's eyes dropped to the half-covered gadget that he carried along with his coat. The tiny neon lamp beneath the glass bull's-eye was flashing a frantic warning.

Captain Zero was immediately behind him.

SCHOENLING HURRIED down the stairs into the total dark of the basement, left hand fumbling into the pocket of the coat he carried to grip the butt of his gun. Once he thought he heard a stealthy, padded step behind him and forced himself to resist the urge to look. What good would it do to look back now?

Scuffling across the concrete floor, Schoenling's left elbow contacted the side of the steam boiler. His left foot, then, must be on the very brink of the cistern. He took a long striding step that cleared the opening and kept on. Not until he had reached the entrance into the fuel cellar did he pause to listen with bated breath, his heart hammering wildly.

No less rapid than the beating of Schoenling's heart were the pulsations of the Geiger counter's signal lamp.

Sound rushed in on silence. At first, a scuff coming up from the floor. Then a hollow echoing cry of terror from the mouth of the cistern. A splash.

Schoenling's indrawn breath came as a sob of sheer relief. He trotted back through the dark, sprang across the opening of the cistern, fanned the air above his head until he located the pull cord of the light and jerked it on. Awed by his own accomplishment, he tiptoed to the edge of the cistern and looked down.

Bubbles winked and burst on the oily surface of the black water five feet below floor level. There were footprints other than Schoenling's in the coal dust, from the foot of the stairs to the brink of the cistern—but no farther. A smile spread across Schoenling's face.

"So much for Captain Zero," he said as he stepped to the front of the boiler to get one of the three heavy oak planks that were used to cover the cistern opening.

When the boards had been replaced, Schoenling put on his coat and carried the Geiger counter openly up the steps and through the trap into his shop. He closed the trap, went back through the connecting door into his office.

There was, unfortunately, Mo Sipes still to be dealt with. Schoenling put the Geiger counter down on his desk and before turning it off noted, to his satisfaction, that the flashes from the signal lamp were much more infrequent. Had there been time, Schoenling would have enjoyed sitting there and watching the glow of the tiny lamp die out altogether.

"Business before pleasure," he muttered as he switched off the Geiger counter. He moved over to the dead man on the floor, hooked puffy hands into Mo Sipes' armpits, and dragged Mo to the right side of the door leading out into the alley.

Schoenling then turned out the light, opened the door, and stepped outside to look in both directions along the narrow canyon between buildings. He then reached in through the door, got Mo by the back of the coat collar and dragged him through the door which he closed behind him.

HE LEFT Mo Sipes near the back door of the tavern on the

corner. The place was dark, closed by the liquor curfew, and it seemed a logical place for Mo Sipes to turn up with a bullet in his head. Schoenling then retraced his steps to halt within three yards of his own back door.

There was somebody there, close to the door and waiting for Schoenling. The fat man's left hand moved to the side pocket of his white suit coat. He peered through the gloom at the shrouded and faceless figure.

The Man in Black. Schoenling took a breath and his hand fell away from his pocket.

"So it's you," he said.

"Me."

"You gave me a bit of a start. I was about to go out to the River House to see the fun."

"I'll go along." The muffled voice was very low, hard to hear. *"I like fun too."*

Schoenling chuckled. "Then you should have been here a moment ago. I've disposed of Captain Zero."

"You've what?"

"You heard what I said. Captain Zero. Drowned. An easy death, I've heard."

"Zero was here?"

"Indeed yes. Ask Mo Sipes—not that you'll get an answer." Schoenling's hand went out to the doorknob. "You'll come in, of course? I've a bit of cleaning up to do before we can go."

"I'll wait here. Don't take too long."

"Suit yourself," Schoenling returned coolly. Having dispatched the vaunted Captain Zero, Schoenling felt a renewal

146

of his self confidence. He was henceforth playing second fiddle to no one—the Man in Black included.

Schoenling entered the office, turned on the light. There was a little blood on the floor at the spot where Mo Sipes' head had been, and this Schoenling carefully wiped up with a cloth. Straightening, he looked at the cloth. That was the trouble with blood—when you cleaned it up you simply transferred it from one object to another. Now he'd have to get rid of the rag.

He started toward the door connecting office and shop, paused, came back to the desk, and picked up the Geiger counter which he switched on. Just to check and double check. He carried the gadget and the rag into the shop and then down through the trap into the basement where he disposed of it in the furnace.

Then he put the Geiger counter down on top of the boards that covered the cistern, crouched there, his eye fixed on the signal lamp. It didn't light—not so much as a feeble glow.

"Well, well," Schoenling said, pleased. He straightened, carried the Geiger counter back upstairs, closed the trap, moved on into the office, turned out the light, and stepped to the door.

The Man in Black was waiting for him beyond the threshold.

"Come along," Schoenling said loftily. He turned to the left and the shrouded figure fell into step beside him.

NED BARDON did not enter his apartment building on Piedmont immediately after putting his car into the garage. With the two packages of stolen securities that Captain Zero had addressed to Chief-of-Police Cavanaugh tucked under his arm, Ned Bardon moved around the back of the building to the southeast corner and then along the narrow walk at the side to gain the street.

His mind had been so thoroughly occupied with other things that he had forgot to post the bonds on his way home. There was a drop box on the next corner which would do as well as any other.

When he had stuffed the bulky packages through the slot, Ned Bardon turned and walked back to the Piedmont entrance of the building. There was a man standing in the vestibule of the apartment building, one shoulder against the mailbox plate, a cigarette smoldering in his short yellow fingers.

He wore loose-fitting gray flannel slacks, a deep green sports shirt, and an Optimo shape straw hat that shadowed the upper part of his face. There was a crescent-shaped scar on his chin like a second mouth, drooping at its extremities and sullen.

Ned Bardon took out his keys and approached the door.

"Mr. Bardon."

Ned Bardon turned, jaw muscles tightening. The short figure in sports clothes leaned away from the wall, tipped back his head to regard Bardon from beneath thick, leathery looking eyelids.

"Yes?" Ned Bardon said. "I don't think I know you."

"Gomez," said the other. "Little Al Gomez. Schoenling wants to see you."

Ned Bardon thrust the proper key into the lock. "Tell Schoenling to go to hell. Right at three A.M. I'm not seeing anybody."

The short fingered hand closed on Ned Bardon's wrist, gently but firmly. Ned Bardon looked at the other man over a shoulder.

"Don't paw me, damn it."

"Then take the key out, Mr. Bardon," Little Al said gently. "Fat Paul is a patient man, but I been waitin' for you for a long time. I didn't have the heart to break in on you and the tomato. If I had a tomato like that I wouldn't want no interruptions. So I been waiting. Fat Paul has been waiting. And now—" Little Al accompanied this with a gesture that casually smoothed the tail of his shirt down over his belly and revealed the shape of a gun which he carried tucked into his belt.

Ned Bardon's mouth quirked. "Like that, huh?"

"Only if you want it like that, Mr. Bardon," Little Al said gently. "I'm asking you. Schoenling is asking you."

Ned Bardon put the keys back into his pocket. He looked uneasily past Little Al and into the deserted street.

"Where's Schoenling?"

"We're going there, Mr. Bardon. I got the car right outside."

"Right," Ned Bardon said. He went out wondering if there was the slightest chance that Schoenling had found out that he was playing both ends against the middle. He wished fervently that he had mailed the two packs of stolen securities at any other box than the one on the corner.

Had Little Al Gomez watched him? Could Little Al possibly have recognized the packages? Ned Bardon thought not. But then he wasn't sure. Al Gomez could have, very easily.

What was it Captain Zero had said about a dark corner?

149

CHAPTER 12
THE COLD, DEADLY DAWN

I T WAS a two-story oblong building of buff brick standing back from a blacktop county road. The neon sign on top of the hip roof was not illuminated and not silhouetted against the horizon either because of the towering willow trees that served as a background along the river's edge.

In a back room, Ned Bardon waited—for Schoenling, maybe. For someone else, maybe. For the head man? He couldn't be sure of anything any more.

Presently there were footsteps along the corridor—a woman's hard high heels tick-tacking along to stop just outside the door. Ned Bardon reached up lazily to the bridge lamp and turned its paper shade so that the glare fell upon the door rather than upon his own face. The door opened and he watched the woman ease into the room, her back to the wood trim. Staring at her, Ned Bardon took a long, slow breath.

She had a kind of beauty but it didn't do anything to him. She was a trifle too round? Or too short? Or her hair was too dark? Her blue eyes too darkly circled? Her lips too full and vividly rouged?

Maybe no to all of those. Maybe she wasn't too anything, but she wasn't Ann and she didn't do anything to him. Not now. Once he'd paid twenty dollars for the use of a portable phonograph with a scratchy needle just to hear her voice played back to him from the wax-covered cardboard disk she'd sent to him overseas. Now she wasn't anything, because of Ann.

He expelled some of the long slow breath and asked, "What are you doing here, Madge?"

There was no lightness in her shrug; she'd tried for lightness and couldn't make it. She moved over in front of him, her too-short skirt swaying. Her red mouth smiled.

"It's my room, Ned."

His right hand stirred in a gesture that indicated the bottle on the bureau. "Have a drink. Little Al's hospitality knows no bounds. They told me to wait here for Schoenling."

"Thanks, Ned," she said huskily and moved over to the bureau.

He heard her pouring whiskey into a glass. Little Madge Murphy. He wondered if she was the one. If she was, then he was sunk. Hell, he remembered, had no fury like a woman scorned. She finished her whiskey, rolled the thick tumbler between her palms, and looked at him. Her eyes were cold. "I want to thank you, Ned."

"Oh, sure!"

"For last night," she said. "Jake Katz might have killed me. He was doped to the gills, and he might have killed me."

The muscles around Ned Bardon's mouth tightened. "You were the one."

He stood, feeling the whiskey in his legs, and stepped over to the bed to stand in front of her. She kept rolling the glass in her hands, her eyes downcast.

"Madge," he said softly. "Look up, Madge."

She looked up. Her eyes were the same—glacial. Her lips were triumphantly smiling.

"You wouldn't do this to me, would you, Madge?"

"Do what?" She appeared puzzled. "Thank you for killing Jake Katz?"

"I didn't kill him."

"Of course not, darling," she mocked. "It isn't killing, is it, unless you use a knife and then twist it in the wound."

He let her go. She was the one, all right. And she was doing this to him because she hated him. Out of all the women in the world, it had to be Madge Murphy.

She was saying, "You were insanely jealous, always—weren't you, Ned darling? And so when you saw me with Jake Katz you hit him with a piece of lead pipe and then you hid the body."

HE STOOD back from her, tall, his face waxy, and a kind of smile on his mouth. He didn't accuse her of lying. He wouldn't give her the satisfaction of watching him rise to hopeless self defense. Because she'd made up her mind she was going to do this to him. She could and she would.

A board creaked, and Ned Bardon glanced toward the door. Schoenling moved ponderously into the room, his face wreathed in smiles.

"Hello, my dear. Hello, Bardon. You've met Miss Murphy, I see. You've met—ha-ha—your Waterloo, shall we say?"

Bardon didn't reply. His eyes strayed from Schoenling's face and into the murky hall beyond. Just outside the door someone watched and listened. A man. Bardon's eyes traveled up from thick-soled shoes with black canvas uppers to a long black rain-coat and thence to a face completely covered in black cloth.

Bardon's mouth fell open and remained that way—dry and

soundless. As he stared at the somber figure in the shadows, he heard Schoenling's voice as though from a vast distance.

"Just in case anything were to happen to the young lady, Bardon, let me remind you that her affidavit describing in some detail how you killed Jake Katz is on file with a certain attorney who would be only too happy to deliver it to the county prosecutor. So if you have the slightest idea that you might be able to silence Miss Murphy—"

Bardon whipped around to face the fat man. "Don't be a bigger fool than God made you," he snapped.

Schoenling's eyebrows peaked in surprise at this outburst.

"I'm not a killer," Ned Bardon said more quietly, "and you damned well know it." He stared at Schoenling for a moment.

Schoenling chuckled. "But of course not, my dear chap." He took Bardon's arm. "You're a dealer in securities, which reminds me that we have some business to discuss. Later, perhaps, if you'd like to continue this interesting discussion with the charming Miss Murphy." And Schoenling conducted Ned Bardon from the room.

Madge stood erect for a moment and stared at the door which had closed on Ned Bardon. Then her shoulders sagged, the thick glass tumbler slipped from her fingers, and she sank down on the edge of the bed. A dry sob broke from her contorted mouth.

She was lying there when the door behind her quietly opened. MADGE TWISTED up, her eyes wide. The man who had entered the room and was now closing the door wore shapeless, ill-fitting garments of black. Shoes, trousers, raincoat, gloves, and hat—all black. Gloves and a raincoat on a night like this?

Madge's lips parted, but her scream lodged in her throat as the man turned and swooped. The face beneath the hat was shrouded in black cloth. Hands covered in black cotton gloves reached for her throat. Madge felt the firm pressure of thumbs and fingers. She closed her eyes.

Ned Bardon

"Don't scream, Miss Murphy."

Scream? She couldn't breath. Blindly she brought her hands up to tear at the gloved fingers.

"You won't scream? Promise?"

Madge's eyelids opened. The shrouded face was close to hers. There were eye-slits in the cloth yet, oddly, she wasn't conscious of eyes at all—only a faint glimmer of reflected light like pin-points.

Madge nodded vigorously, and the pressure of the gloved fingers relaxed slowly. She gasped for breath. The hands dropped to her shoulders and shook her briskly.

"Listen to me, Miss Murphy. That affidavit you signed—where is it? With what attorney is it filed? Quickly, Miss Murphy."

She got air down into her lungs—not far down but far enough to speak.

"Why do you want to know? Who are you?"

"Because it can kill Bardon. You understand that, don't you? That paper you signed can kill him. You loved him once, remember? If he's tried and convicted for murder on the evidence which you've fabricated, then you will have killed him."

"Who—who are you?" she stammered. "What are you doing here?" And then, on sudden impulse, she got her right hand up between his arms, caught the fullness of black cloth that hung down from the sweatband of the hat, and tore it away.

And then she screamed—screamed and broke away. Stark terror gave her strength. She outstripped him to the door, got through, yanked on the knob and fumbled at the key. For an instant the narrowing aperture revealed the hideous secret behind the mask.

He hadn't any face. No face at all. No head. No anything between hat brim and shoulders.

She had the door closed, the key twisted in the lock. The knob was wrenched from her grasp, but that didn't matter now. The door was locked. The faceless one couldn't reach her. Now she was all right. Now she could scream and scream again....

On the opposite side of the door, Captain Zero, a seemingly headless apparition in misfit clothes of black, strode to the single window and started to knock out the screen with repeated blows of his gloved hands. And then he noticed the wrought iron grill.

"Damn!" he said quietly, succinctly.

Somewhere beyond the dark the crowing of a rooster brought

the gravity of his situation home with all the subtlety of a hard blow to the midsection. The early summer dawn was approaching on swift gray wings.

With it would come the visible substance of Lee Allyn.

CHAPTER 13
GALLERY OF ROGUES

"OH, SHADDUP!" somebody shouted at Madge Murphy from behind a door along the narrow corridor. Screams were not unusual in River House, nothing to get excited about. But Madge ran on down the hall, screaming. She was near the stairs leading into the garage when a door behind her opened.

"Miss Murphy—"

She turned, wild-eyed, as Schoenling sidled out into the hall. She fled to him, and she screamed again. Schoenling caught her by an arm and slapped her sharply across the side of the face.

"Stop that!"

She stopped. Panting, she rolled her eyes toward the room at the end of the hall. "That man—" She ran a hand over her face, unable to say more at the moment.

"I thought you were a sensible girl," Schoenling chided. "That man happens to be my partner. If he chooses to cover his face with a piece of black cloth, that's his business." He chuckled. "Though I admit that's hardly the way to go calling on a lady."

Now she could speak. Now she could tell him why she had screamed.

"His face—he doesn't have any."

"Oh, come now!"

"No, he hasn't!" She stamped her foot. "Go and see for yourself. I locked him in there. *And he hasn't any face!*"

"Nonsense, my girl." Schoenling strode buoyantly down the hall to the door at the end of the room, but as his right hand went out to turn the key in the lock, his left dipped into the side pocket of his coat where he carried his little gun.

There was, from Schoenling's viewpoint, no one in the room at all. There were clothes on the bed—black trousers, hat, gloves and raincoat—and on the door near the edge of the bed a pair of black canvas shoes with thick crepe rubber soles rested at odd angles to one another. Schoenling frowned.

He approached the bed warily, his eyes on the shoes. *He* had a pair of shoes exactly like that, which was odd in the extreme because he distinctly remembered having had the brown canvas uppers dyed black.

Schoenling was on the verge of stooping to pick up one of the shoes when it leaped up from the floor and kicked him very hard in the belly. Schoenling backed fast, but his feet couldn't keep up with his center of gravity. He sat down hard on the floor, his startled eyes protruding somewhat from their puffy lids, his mouth open and gasping.

Shoes—the room seemed to be filled with shoes. One of them sailed through the air, end over end, straight for Schoenling's head. Schoenling unlimbered his gun and fired at it. The shoe struck the wall above his head and fell a few feet from him.

But the second shoe was bounding across the floor exactly as though somebody was wearing it. And before Schoenling could draw a bead on it he was faced with trouble of another sort. Something hit him in the face and flattened him. Something else, unseen and formless, landed on top of him.

His gun seemed to come alive in his grasp, for it writhed and twisted and finally spun out of his hand. Invisible fingers clawed into his scant hair. His head was raised, slammed back against the floor, raised and slammed down again.

And darkness closed over him....

Captain Zero stood, breathing heavily. He kicked off the one remaining shoe. As he picked up Schoenling's gun he noticed with a cold jab of fear that he was becoming faintly visible—as gray and wraithlike as a wisp of smoke, but visible nevertheless.

He spun to the bed and snatched up the black trousers. With these trailing over his left arm, he jerked the door open and stepped into the long corridor. Orange-red gunflame jetted from a partially open door. A bullet tugged at the flying trousers. Zero swung Schoenling's gun and fired into the narrow opening as he passed. Glancing back he saw Little Gomez wallow out of the room on caving knees, both hands over his face and screaming horribly.

Zero reached the stairs. Two shots clipped the wall above his head and showered him with plaster dust. Halfway down the stairs, he leaped to the garage floor, sprinted out into the gray morning, and headed for the nearest car—the one which had brought Little Al and Ned Bardon to the River House. The ignition key was in the lock.

Zero pitched the black clothing in onto the seat, got in under the wheel. The hand that went out to the switch showed each bone in clearly defined silhouette.

WHEN DORO KELLY entered the *World* office at her usual time that Tuesday morning, she ran into Mr. Fairish at the door of the city room. Something about the red-haired city editor's attitude suggested that he had been waiting there especially to pounce on her.

"Lovely, haughty Lady Kelly," said Mr. Fairish, "I crave a boon. Will you lend me your ear and possibly your eye for about five seconds?" And Fairish brought forth a rolled paper which he opened and flaunted in front of Doro's face.

"Oh, the *Sentinel*."

"Oh, yes, the *Sentinel*," Fairish echoed. "Will you cast a glance at column four of the *Sentinel*?"

Doro Kelly frowned at column four and read aloud: " 'Jake Katz Murdered. Body Of Jessop Street Hoodlum Found In Auto Junk Yard.'" And there was a picture of the late Mr. Katz—a dark, dissolute appearing young man, much too smooth an article to be actually handsome.

Doro Kelly looked at Mr. Fairish's inflamed face. "That's the story Lee was on. Where is he?"

Fairish nodded repeatedly. "Well may you ask. Believe it or not, Allyn went out of here yesterday morning, following what he claimed was an exclusive tip that Jake Katz had been murdered. Allyn was to get verification. That was yesterday morning, I repeat. And since that time I have neither seen Allyn nor heard from him."

"Poor Mr. Fairish," said Doro with no discernible sympathy.

" 'He doesn't 'phone, he doesn't write, and I'm alone most every night—'"

"Oh, shut up!" Fairish wadded the Sentinel and threw it to the floor. "Scooped, by gad! He had the ball in his hands, and he fumbled. I swear I don't know whether I'm running a newspaper here or a house of mystery. People come here for employment, they vanish from the face of the earth, and nobody every hears from them again including their unfortunate employer."

"People?" Doro's glance skipped from desk to desk. No one seemed to be conspicuously absent, among the staff members, except Lee Allyn.

"Yes, people. That Poynter kid. She, I thought, had enthusiasm. Nothing else—just enthusiasm which, when it is fresh and new, will sometimes bring out a reporter. Or so I thought."

"Poynter, Poynter," Doro Kelly muttered and then remembered the fluffy little blonde in pink who had been trying to land a job on the *World*. Sweet Alice Poynter, the Darling Girl Reporter.

Doro looked sharply at the city editor. "Oh, but you couldn't," she said, aghast. "Sweet Alice majored in journalism. You couldn't have broken your cardinal rule, Mr. Fairish. For the sake of a pretty face and a well-turned ankle?"

"Well, I—" Fairish scratched the back of his head in an effort to conceal his embarrassment. "The kid had a lot of determination and I thought I'd give her a chance. Especially inasmuch as she came to me with a pretty good idea for a feature. I told her to take a whirl at it, and if it turned out okay I half promised to find a spot for her somewhere. And what happens?" Fairish waved his arms. "Pffft! She vanishes."

"This feature Sweet Alice was going to do," she began casually, "is it anything I would be interested in?"

"I don't think so," Fairish said dryly. "It had to do with romance."

"What kind of romance?"

"Is there another kind? Boy meets girl." Fairish shrugged. "This was boy meets girl—through a professional introductory service which is operating here in Pendleville."

"You mean one of those mail-order things for lonely hearts?" Doro persisted.

Howie Myers

"I don't know. It was Miss Poynter's idea. She was going to register with this outfit, take a grab-bag date, and see what came of it. It's still a good idea, either as a human interest bit or as an exposé if it's as crummy as it could be. I was hoping I'd have something out of it I could put on page one of section two, but maybe we can drum up something else."

Doro Kelly helped herself to one of Mr. Fairish's cigarettes and permitted him to light it for her.

"You know, you're a sweet old grouch," she said archly, "and not anywhere near as clever as you think you are. I'll take that job, Mr. F."

Fairish grunted. "Then hop to it. What are you waiting for—an engraved invitation? It's called Miss Prudence's Introductory Service, and the address is 1924 East Twenty-second."

"Miss Prudence," Doro mused. "I like that, don't you?" As she moved away she added, "I hope it's crummy."

Fairish admitted that he hoped so too.

The outward appearance of 1924 East Twenty-second suggested crumminess. I was a two-story frame building with blistered gray paint and a weary looking front porch where a sign advertising furnished rooms hung lopsidedly from a turned pillar.

Doro managed to reduce her usual self-reliant knock to something suggesting timidity, and the door was presently opened by a tiny woman in red lounging pajamas whose close-cropped gray hair resembled very fine steel wool. She was anywhere from forty to sixty years old, sharp featured, with a pair of eyes that any mackerel would inevitably have been caught dead with.

"I—uh," began Doro.

"Come in, come in, my dear." Miss Prudence skipped back from the wide open door and her lacquer-tipped toes wriggled joyously in a pair of girlish sandals. "Sit down, honey. I'll have the fan going in a minute. It's warm, but then I dress for it."

Doro stepped into a shabby room where there was a couch,

two chairs, straight and easy, and an ancient roll-top desk. She sat down hesitantly on the end of the couch nearest the desk while Miss Prudence plugged in an eight-inch electric fan.

"There," said Miss Prudence gayly, "that's better, isn't it?"

The fan was kicking up a great deal of noise and very little air, but Doro agreed that it was better. Miss Prudence darted to the desk, alighted on the edge of the chair and swiveled it around with a fine display of energy to face her prospective client.

Miss Prudence's smile showed excellent dentures and left her eyes strictly alone—stone cold dead in the market. Doro lowered her gaze demurely and picked her fingers.

"I—I don't know just how to begin," she said.

"Of course you don't, honey," said Miss Prudence, literally brimming over with understanding. "That's just the trouble—you don't know how to begin. It's all so strange and new and all, and while you undoubtedly have met some young men here in our fair city, they haven't been quite... the... type. Now isn't that it, huhn? And you're just a weeney bit lonely."

MISS PRUDENCE opened a drawer and whipped out a small white file card. "Your name, please?" And when Doro had told her, Miss Prudence wrote *Dora Kelley* in a round, school-girlish hand. She then subjected Doro to some keen scrutiny and nodded in approval.

"Brunette," she said, writing.

Doro, who was properly an Irish blonde, nevertheless permitted herself to be catalogued as a brunette. She gave her weight and her height—"that's for dancing, you know," Miss Prudence explained—and opened her purse to procure the four dollar registration fee.

"And do you happen to have a snapshot?" Miss Prudence asked. "I don't always ask, but in your case I think it would be an excellent idea. And if you'll excuse me a moment, I'll just put on my earrings."

Miss Prudence was up and away, but never far away, chattering happily all the while. "I feel positively naked without my earrings. Do you, dearie? But then you don't need anything of the sort, I suppose. It would be gilding the lily."

Doro, who was searching her purse for a photograph of herself, glanced up and over her shoulder. Miss Prudence was putting on an earring, but she was also looking down into Doro's open purse, undoubtedly estimating how much good she could do in the world—for herself. Then Miss Prudence flitted around to the desk again, took the photo, and compared it with the original.

"Doesn't flatter you a bit. In fact— Wasn't that the 'phone?"

Doro had heard no 'phone possibly because of the racket from the electric fan, but she was glad enough to have Miss Prudence fly out into the hall for a moment. Doro leaned forward, flipped up the top of the card file on the desk, and began digging.

There was no card for Alice Poynter among the P's. Sweet Alice's wholesome face turned up among the J's listed as Mary Jones, which was quite original of her. Doro was thumbing back through the H's when she came across another face that was familiar, though only vaguely so.

A dark, dissolutely handsome young man whose name was—

164

Robert Harbin? Doro didn't think so. When she finally placed the face in her memory file it was that of the late Jake Katz— the identical picture, in fact, which had been reproduced on the front page of the *Sentinel*.

"Oh, my dear!" Miss Prudence, a darting tanager, was in the room, at the desk in time to snatch the file case beyond Doro's grasp. Miss Prudence's laughter was a bit strained. "That's last year's file, dearie. Income tax, you know. They're always a year or so behind. Can't have you setting your dear young heart on some man who's passé, can we?"

Doro Kelly couldn't think of a better word to describe Jake Katz, alias Robert Harbin, than passé.

She said faintly, "Oh."

"You can't possible imagine who that was on the 'phone just now. A perfectly charming young man. *And* very comfortably fixed financially, I might add. And I said to myself, 'He certainly must meet Miss Shelley.'"

"Kelly."

"Yes, Kelly. I've so many girls, you know. And he's on his way over here right now, my dear. Can you imagine?"

Doro couldn't imagine. She didn't even want to imagine. She stood.

"I really have to be going now. Perhaps—well, if he likes my picture—"

"Oh, won't you stay just a few minutes, dearie?" Miss Prudence urged. "He lives just around the corner." The inconsistency of his living just around the corner from here and being "very comfortably fixed financially" apparently didn't bother her in the least. "We'll just finish filling out your card, and then by that time, possibly he'll be here. What's your 'phone number, honey?" DORO KELLY gave her telephone number. "And I really must fly," she added, backing to the door. "If he likes my picture—this young man—well, I—I—"

"You'll consider it," concluded Miss Prudence. "Of course. No obligation at all. No obligation on anybody's part, including mine, I always say." She was pursuing Doro Kelly into the hall. She was trying to hold Doro with everything she had short of actual physical restraint. Opportunity, she insisted, might very well be knocking at Miss Kelly's door.

Miss Kelly, by this time, was at the foot of the shabby stairway, her back to opportunity and possibly something much less attractive. She had hold of something, she knew, and now that she had it she wasn't at all sure what she was going to do with it. That Sweet Alice Poynter might have had hold of the same thing before her unexplained disappearance, was not a reassuring thought.

Doro got into her Plymouth coupé and drove a little way up the street before she decided it mightn't be a bad idea to wait around and watch for this "charming young man" to enter 1924.

She had no way of knowing, of course, that the charming young man had already gone into the building by the back door. Although he had dyed his hair a rather alarming shade of red and had shaved off his mustache, following the bank stick-up on the previous day, Charles "Duke" Laymon preferred back doors whenever available. He stood now in Miss Prudence's office, a compact man in a neat brown tropic worsted suit.

"Schoenling said you'd 'phoned," he said. "Where is she?"

Miss Prudence wrung thin fingers. "She left. I couldn't stop her."

Duke Laymon flared his nostrils in the manner of George Raft whom he fancied he resembled. "The hell you couldn't."

"But look," said Miss Prudence excitedly and waved the file card on "Dora Kelley" under the charming young man's nose. "I've got everything here—her picture, description. And here's her 'phone number. She's a reporter for the *World*. I saw a press card in her purse. Schoenling said if any reporter or cop came—"

"Sure, sure," Laymon interrupted "You was to stall 'em off until somebody came here to take care of 'em. You didn't do that. Gimme." The charming young man jerked the cards from Miss Prudence's fingers. He then picked up Doro Kelly's card. He looked at the pictures of the two girls for a long time.

"Too bad," he said. "The reporter—she have a car?"

"Yes. A gray Plymouth coupé."

Duke Laymon had Doro Kelly's picture in his hand and he was looking at it as he went out. "Too bad," he said again.

CHAPTER 14
#4 ON THE MURDER PARADE

LEE ALLYN sat at the side of the desk in Chief-of-Police Ed Cavanaugh's office and helped himself from the tray of food that Cavanaugh had ordered sent in. It was lunch for Cavanaugh and breakfast for Allyn.

"I thought I had it made last night," Allyn said between gulps of steaming coffee. "I had Schoenling foxed into thinking I was dead. And then with some clothing I found around the pawnshop and a piece of black cloth I ripped from an umbrella, I fixed myself up like the masked marvel who's directing operations of the mob. And where did I land? Up a blind alley as usual."

Cavanaugh conveyed a forkfull of apple pie to his mouth, worked it into his cheek, and asked, "How in the hell does an invisible man kid anybody into thinking he's dead—that's what I'd like to know."

Allyn laughed. "Though," he said, "it was very unfunny last night. I slipped into the pawnshop office with Mo Sipes. When Schoenling went upstairs it began to look as though I'd have to intervene to prevent Mo from killing the fat man.

"Mo and Zero tussled a bit, and when Mo's gun went off it was pointing the wrong way, from his viewpoint. Schoenling got wise to Zero's presence—a Geiger counter was responsible, I think—and thought he could pull off a fast one. He lured me down into a very dark cellar where Schoenling had previously taken the top off a cistern.

"I was supposed to follow him and fall into the cistern. The joker was, of course, that nobody had ever informed Schoenling that Captain Zero had been totally blind for a good part of his life. I could smell the cistern and hear the hollow sound Schoenling's footsteps made.

"When I got to the edge of the cistern, I groped around a bit for something that I could toss into the water. There was a coal scoop leaning against the furnace. I dropped that into the cistern, and then made sure that I didn't leave any footprints in the coal dust that would lead away from the trap I was supposed to have fallen into."

"How'd you manage that—avoiding the footprints?" Cavanaugh asked.

"Some convenient water pipes overhead. I just hung onto them until Schoenling got out of the cellar. Later, when he was disposing of Mo Sipes' body, I put the fritz on Schoenling's Geiger counter just in case he decided to do any double-checking."

The two men ate in silence for a moment, and then Cavanaugh wadded his paper napkin and reached for a cigarette. He studied Allyn through frankly suspicious eyes.

"You mean you went through all that and didn't come up with any information I can use?"

"That's right. I wormed my way into what looked like the middle of things, and it turned out to be another blind alley."

"You didn't learn anything at all, huh?"

"Only that Bardon has an old flame named Madge Murphy, and they are definitely *not* that way about each other anymore. Oddly, though," Allyn added thoughtfully, "the first time I called on Bardon, he had a disk on his record player which I'm sure was a recording of Madge's voice. It was one of those lovey-dovey things the girls used to send to the boys overseas."

"What's that got to do with anything?"

Allyn shrugged. "You asked what I found out, and I told you. I can't help it if this case has so many sideroads that we can't find the main thoroughfare. You got the stolen securities all right, didn't you?"

Cavanaugh nodded. "In the mail. Thanks."

"You'll keep it quiet?"

CAVANAUGH STARED at the slight blond man. "Keep it quiet? What would I want to do that for? With both newspapers yelping about police incompetence, you've got to show some tangible results."

"Oh, lord," Allyn breathed. He put down his coffee cup. "Who'd you give the handout to—Doro Kelly?"

"I haven't seen Doro," Cavanaugh returned peevishly. "I gave it to Wilson on your sheet and also a man from the *Sentinel*. What's wrong with that, Allyn? I don't get it at all."

Allyn shook his head repeatedly back and forth. "Not good, Ed. Not your fault, of course. I ought to have been down here earlier, but I guess I overslept." He had had exactly four hours of sleep that morning and, of course, none the night before.

"But what's wrong with it?" Cavanaugh persisted, now thoroughly alarmed.

"Look, where do you suppose I got those securities?"

Cavanaugh hadn't thought much about that. "I supposed you picked them up when you were at Schoenling's."

"Bardon gave them to me. To Captain Zero, that is. Bardon has been working with Zero."

Cavanaugh pushed the lunch tray aside and rested his forearms on the desk.

"Now wait a minute," he said quietly. "Bardon has been working for you. You got the securities from Bardon. Now, where the hell did Bardon get them?"

"From Schoenling." Under Cavanaugh's intense stare, Allyn squirmed in his chair. "And you know damned well where Schoenling got them."

"But *how* did Bardon get them?"

"Schoenling picked Bardon to push the hot stuff. Bardon pretended to fall in with the scheme, turned the securities over to me as soon as he got his hands on them. Is that clear?"

"Clear?" Cavanaugh snorted. And then he jumped to the inevitable and correct conclusion. "What's Schoenling got on Bardon?"

"Well, now he's got plenty on him," Allyn said evasively. "Now that you gave that handout to the papers."

Cavanaugh said, "You know what I mean. What did he have on him in the first place? Look, you're a jewel thief and you've got a pocketful of hot ice. You don't walk into Tiffany's with it and ask the proprietors to turn it over for you because you've heard that Tiffany makes a nice piece of change."

"No, you don't," Allyn admitted uncomfortably. "You know this whole thing could be a con game—a variation of the Spanish prisoner gag, only based on the fact that one of the Reynox Company's stockholders disappeared in South America some time ago."

Allyn repeated his conclusions which had come out of his conversation with Bardon on the previous night. Cavanaugh listened closely, nodding now and then.

"That's pretty good," the chief said. "Reynox stock, as I understand it, would sell at a premium if there was any of it available. The con would offer spurious certificates at a discount, all very hush-hush under the pretext of raising a ransom for this Reynox man who is, presumably, being held prisoner by some South American crowd.

"The con could always say that if the matter became known to the public it might result in an unpleasant international situation—not to mention death for the imprisoned Reynox official."

"And it fits in beautifully with the Bachelors' Club angle," Allyn contributed. "Those old men are perfect victims, all alone in the world, nobody to worry about what they do with their money or what becomes of it after they're gone. And if any one of them exhibited too much curiosity, he could be knocked off, the spurious Reynox securities stolen and destroyed. And, incidentally, Bardon mentioned that Duncan Moore had questioned Bardon's boss Mr. Cline, in a roundabout manner, about Reynox stock."

CAVANAUGH NODDED, his face impassive. "I'll buy that con game angle, Lee. At least I'll make a down payment on it. And I'll find out if any other members of the Bachelors' Club have been approached by some purveyor of supposed Reynox stock. I'll find out this afternoon. Now to get back to Ned Bardon—"

"Yeah," Allyn interrupted, "I'd better check with him. Bardon was still at the River House last night when I checked out in somewhat of a rush. If I can use your 'phone."

Cavanaugh waved his hand generously to indicate the outside 'phone, but there was a gleam in his eyes as he watched Allyn locate the telephone number of Earhart & Cline in the directory. Allyn dialed, got the switchboard at the investment house where he caught Ned Bardon on the way out to lunch. There was a moment's pause while Bardon returned to his office.

"Okay," Bardon's voice came guardedly from the receiver.

"This is Zero," Allyn said. "How did you make out last night?"

"I'm in," Bardon replied. "Here's a tip for what it's worth. George Rumpler is next."

"Rumpler?" Allyn frowned.

"The Bachelors' Club. Rumpler is the one who is blind."

"Thanks, Bardon, And watch your step. There's been a leak here at headquarters."

"Meaning, I shouldn't start to read any continued stories?" was Bardon's morose question.

"Meaning stay away from fat men," Allyn concluded and hung up. He turned to find Cavanaugh with a slight smile on his usually expressionless face.

"Rumpler is slated as Number Four on the murder parade," Allyn said.

Cavanaugh nodded. "I'll have men watching every one of those old duffers. And now, to get back to Bardon. What's Schoenling got against him?"

Allyn said, "I think this is where I came in," and started for the door.

"I'll find out," Cavanaugh promised.

"You probably will."

But it would take a little time.

CHAPTER 15
AMONG THE MISSING....

A PERCEPTIBLE hush spread over the *World* city room when Lee Allyn entered, and he was uncomfortably aware of a number of eyes following him as he sought out Fairish. The red-haired city editor was bending over Wilson's desk, talking to Wilson. Fairish gave Allyn a glance, but that was all until Allyn nipped Fairish's shirt sleeve.

"Where's Miss Kelly?" Allyn asked.

"I think she's got herself in a jam of some kind," Fairish said.

Lee Allyn's mouth was momentarily slack.

"What do you mean? What kind of a jam? What'd she say?"

"She said, 'I found Jake Katz's picture and Alice Poynter's in the same file,' and then she hung up. Or somebody hung up for her. I thought maybe she'd 'phone back, but she hasn't."

"Poynter?" Allyn repeated vaguely. "Oh, that's the little blonde who wanted a job. What about her?"

"I gave her a tentative assignment, against my better judgment and she—" Fairish waved his hands—"disappeared. It was an idea for a feature she'd drummed up on a woman who calls herself Miss Prudence and runs a romance racket over on Twenty-second. When Poynter didn't show up, I gave the job to Kelly. Now comes the cut-off 'phone call, and I don't like it."

Allyn said. "I don't like that Jake Katz angle. Lemme have that address on Twenty-second, Fairish. And the Poynter girl's too, if you've got it. Then I'm off to the races."

Allyn braked the car in front of the gray two-story frame

house on Twenty-second Street. He got out, a slight blond man, currently cat-nerved and in a foul mood. He strode up onto the sagging porch, found the stairway, and followed the cardboard arrows to Miss Prudence's door which stood wide open.

A small electric fan on the floor was making a lot of noise, and the little woman in scarlet pajamas doing her nails at the desk wasn't aware of Allyn's presence until he slapped the top of the card filing case with his hand.

Miss Prudence dropped her emery board and spun around in her chair. Her vicious little face was caught naked and she confusedly pulled on her smile.

"Heavens, you scared me, young man!"

The pale blue eyes back of the thick lensed glasses were very nearly as cold as her own. The young man shook his head.

"Huh uh. You don't know what it is to be scared—yet."

The smile drooped to half mast over the shiny dentures. "What's wrong with you, laddy? Did you get a date here or something, and she's giving you a hard time? If that's what it is, remember our responsibility ends with the introduction."

"Skip it," Allyn said. "I've never dated anybody through your bureau, you know it, and you're going to have to accept a lot of responsibility before I'm through with you. Now that you've got that under your wig, maybe you'll give me a few straight answers to a few very straight questions."

"Huh!" said Miss Prudence, perching defiantly on the edge of her chair. "Hear the boy talk."

"There was a girl in here a while ago. Her name is Kelly. She's tall, has dark hair—"

MISS PRUDENCE was emphatically shaking her head. "You had your video tuning in on the wrong channel, boy. There's been no girl, short or tall, come in here all day. Most of my business is carried on through the mail, though I do try to accommodate some of the local young people. You put that down!"

Lee Allyn had picked up the card file. Miss Prudence had popped to her sandaled feet.

"You haven't any right to break in here and start nosing into my private affairs!" she screamed at him. "And I'm going to call the police." She headed for the door into the hall and paused expectantly.

"Well?" he asked dryly. "Why don't you do that? Ask for Cavanaugh. He's a friend of mine, and he sometimes entertains the delusion that he's going to marry the girl I just mentioned."

Miss Prudence moistened her painted lips. She watched Allyn open the card file.

"All right," she said lightly, "you go right ahead and snoop. It's not as though I had anything to hide—it's the principle of the thing. My business is an open book. You're perfectly welcome to look at anything you want."

She sounded pretty sure of herself, and Allyn's heart sank. Whatever it was that Doro Kelly had turned up had probably been well taken care of by now. And Doro—? That he dared not think about. He started going carefully through the file.

Miss Prudence took a cigarette, scratched a match for it on the sole of a sandal, and then fell to pacing back and forth across the little room. Allyn didn't pay too much attention to her.

He didn't, in fact, give her the attention she deserved for, when he was about to return the file to the desk, he discovered her standing opposite him, her smile as phony as her teeth, and a small blue automatic in her right fist.

He was jumpy, and he threw the card file at her without thinking. She ducked, and while the missile was a good yard off target, so was the bead of her gun. Allyn sprang around the desk, caught her wrist, twisted the gun out of her grasp.

His fingers dug into a skinny shoulder, and she was suddenly an old woman, crying piteously. He wouldn't have thought it possible, but there were great tears eroding her crusted makeup. Allyn raised the gun, his expression void of sympathy.

"Don't—" she protested weakly.

"Okay. If you don't want this all mixed up with your hair-do, you'll talk."

"I will," she whimpered sniffling. "I promise."

Allyn nodded toward the card file. "Jake Katz was in that file, wasn't he? Or maybe he called himself Robert Harbin."

Miss Prudence shook her head. "Go ahead and beat me, but I never heard of either of them."

"Alice Poynter," he said, his eyes hard.

"Never heard of her either."

"Nor Schoenling?"

"N-n-nor whoever you said."

"Oh, hell!" Allyn pushed her into the chair. She was lying and they both knew it. She was more afraid of somebody else than she was of Lee Allyn. He wondered how afraid she was of the police. He said, "I think I'll just ring Cavanaugh," and started for the door.

She didn't stop him. She just sat there in the chair and sniffled. He went out into the corridor, kept the gun in his hand while he slotted a nickel and dialed police headquarters.

"This is Allyn, of the *World*," he said, "and I got trouble. Can I speak to Cavanaugh?"

But Cavanaugh wasn't there.

Lee Allyn stood, his shoulder
blades braced against the wall.

CAVANAUGH, AT the moment, was standing in the comfortable lounge of the Bachelors' Club—an old red brick residence on Sixth Street that the gentlemen had purchased some years before when their members had numbered eight.

Now there were but five. Five? Cavanaugh halted in the cased opening, the eyes in his dark expressionless face moving slowly about the big room. Near an open window where a faint hot breeze stirred the curtains, Walter Bedlows of the bald head

"How you want to take it?" Mo Sipes asked.

and pointed ears was absorbed in a game of chess with a fragile, silver-haired man who wore a flowing blue tie as proper background for his Van Dyke beard.

In leather chairs before the empty fireplace, a plump, soft-looking person in a mouse-brown toupe was talking earnestly in a low voice to a gaunt, gnarled fellow who was absently polishing the bowl of his briar pipe on the side of his nose. That made four. Where was the fifth—the one who was blind?

"Where's George Rumpler?" Cavanaugh asked uneasily.

Spencer said, "Rumpler checked out of Hotel Lester, where he's been living for the past ten years, at eight o'clock last night. Ten years, mind you, and he stalked off without saying a word to the manager as to why he was leaving or where he was going."

Cavanaugh said grimly, "I wish you'd let me know about this earlier." According to the tip that Lee Allyn had got from Bardon, George Rumpler was next on the murder schedule. It might be a red herring. It might not. But Rumpler's disappearance didn't help matters any. If he had disappeared, he was probably in danger of his life....

FORTY MILES west of the city, the flat prairie land was bordered by a range of rugged hills that had been left untouched by the great Glacier. There were deep ravines, jagged outcroppings of stone, and the thinly populated area had largely grown up in hardwood forest.

Remote from the highway and straddling a hog-backed ridge, there was a summer cabin constructed of rough-sawed oak. Land's End was the name of the place, and here George

Rumpler sat in a high-backed rocker on the screened porch. It was cool there because of the shade, because rising thermals from the valley created a turbulence in the air.

Rumpler rocked back and forth on the porch and smiled. It had been a good many years since he'd sat in a rocker—so long that he'd forgot what a simple pleasure it was just to sit and tip back and forth, back and forth.

I believe I'll just try and buy this rocker, he thought. Take it back with me. It'll probably look odd in a hotel room, but who cares. *I* won't be looking at it.

And then it occurred to him that he might be able to buy not only the rocker but this cabin. He liked it here. The clean fresh air, the smell of woods-mold, the fragrance of growing things, and all of the bird sounds which he had actually forgotten existed. He liked it, and he felt safe.

If there was really someone who was trying to wipe out the Bachelors' Club members one at a time, then he, George Rumpler, stood an excellent chance of surviving. Beside Standish, his servant who had accompanied him here, there was only one other person who knew where George Rumpler was, and that person he could trust implicitly.

"Standish," the blind man called, "what are we having for supper? This air has given me an appetite like a horse."

There was no answer, and Rumpler recalled that he had heard the kitchen screen door slam a little while ago. Standish had probably gone down to the spring for water. That was one thing that would have to be done if he decided to buy this little hilltop hide-away—there'd have to be water piped up from the spring. Water and plumbing and a good furnace.

Rumpler's day-dreaming was interrupted by footsteps coming up from the lane. No car had approached, so the steps must be those of Standish. And yet, if Standish had gone down to the spring he would hardly approach the cabin from this direction. Rumpler's smile faded as the footsteps came up the porch stairs.

"Standish?" he said timidly.

"Oh, no—not that. Don't tell me I'm beginning to sound like Standish," a familiar voice spoke.

"Hel-lo!" Rumpler's smile of welcome was wide. He put out a groping hand which was clasped in that of his visitor. "I can't tell you how delighted I am you found this hide-away for me. I've been hoping you'd drop in. Notice how cool it is. I had the best night's sleep I've had in an age."

The hand was withdrawn from his.

"That's fine. You did everything I told you to, did you?"

"Oh, yes." Rumpler chuckled. "Not a soul knows. As to the contents of my safety deposit box, Standish sleeps on it every night. I'd trust him above steel and locks, especially with those bandits about, looting one vault after another."

"That's fine," the other said, and Rumpler heard the footsteps leave the porch and enter the living room.

"Notice that bedroom, will you?" Rumpler called. "Standish has the cot, and at night he pulls it across the door. He actually does. And he's got an old Army pistol."

"Yes, you've got it made," the other said, returning to the porch. "And what a view from here."

RUMPLER'S SMILE became a trifle sad. "Is there? Tell me about it, can you? I asked Standish to describe it and he said, 'Trees. Just trees.'"

"Well, that's about right. Hills covered with trees. Down there in the valley there's a little patch of a field that must be four or five miles away. From here it looks a lot like a putting green on a golf course, but it's probably—"

"Where's your car?" Rumpler suddenly interrupted.

"Down on the highway. I wasn't sure I could make it."

"Standish didn't have a particle of trouble. You mean you walked all the way up here from the highway?"

"That's right. I thought you wanted me to describe the view to you."

"Yes," Rumpler replied, a note of uneasiness in his voice. "But I didn't understand about the car. It seems odd anybody would walk so far uphill on a day like this. Where are you now?"

"The car, you mean? I just told you."

"No, you— You're standing behind me, aren't you?" The blind man tipped forward in the rocker. He said pettishly, "I never like to have people stand behind me."

"Well, you see I can do what I've got to do so much better when I'm behind you."

"Do?" Rumpler gasped. "What are you going to do?"

"Just hold still now. This isn't going to hurt at all, old man."

Sudden panic gripped the blind man. He tried to struggle up from the chair, but something cool and soft struck him in the face and forced him back. And the cool soft something molded itself to the contours of his face.

183

He couldn't breath. He couldn't cry out. It's a pillow, he thought, and this is perfectly ridiculous. With a pillow? It could happen to a baby, but not a full grown man!

Yet it was happening to him. He knew it now, with his heart thundering in his ears, he knew it. His feet began kicking a frantic tattoo on the floorboards, but then his friend the murderer simply tipped the rocking chair back far enough so that Rumpler couldn't reach the floor. Rumpler's legs thrashed at the air. His body writhed, but strong arms and the stout wood of the chair held him viselike.

And suddenly all things were clear to him—why he was dying, why the others had died. It had been a childishly simple swindle, and perhaps that was why he was dying like a child, smothered by a pillow.

It was fully two minutes after all signs of resistance had ceased that the murderer removed the pillow from the blind man's face. Rumpler was quite dead, there in the chair. The killer took hold of the knobs on the high back of the chair and worked it to the door connecting the porch and the living room, then over the sill and clear of the door.

With the door closed, the killer went through Rumpler's pockets, came up with a leather key case, then moved on into the adjoining bedroom to the cot where the servant Standish had slept on the night before. There was a flat steel strongbox under the servant's pillow, and from this the killer removed a thick sheaf of stock certificates, went through them carefully, separating those designated as "Reynox Perferred" from the rest which were left in the box.

The Reynox stock was wadded into a ball, dropped onto the middle of the cot, and the whole lavishly doused with kerosene. The murderer struck a match, tossed it onto the cot, turned swiftly, and left the room.

CHAPTER 16
THE HIGHWAY TO HELL

DORO KELLY stared straight ahead through the bug-spotted windshield of the Plymouth. She was as far over on the right side of the cushion as the door would allow. The door was locked on the outside—she'd discovered that many miles back. *He* had taken every precaution. *He* hadn't relaxed for an instant, though his attitude behind the wheel suggested relaxation—right hand steering easily, the left in his lap, fingers lightly closed on the butt of the snub-nosed automatic pistol that pointed in her direction, smoking the lipstick stained cigarette he'd made her light for him.

He'd told her to call him Duke, but she had other names for him—unprintable, not ladylike. A few hours with Duke, and you were a wild thing, obedient and afraid, yet tensely waiting for the opportunity to claw and bite and even to kill him.

It would come—that opportunity. It *had* to come.

He was a compact figure of a man, neat in his brown suit and snap-brim straw. He had a smooth, well-fed look about his face, the beginning of tom-cat jowls. A deceptive softness—even his hands looked soft, and yet how hard they were.

She'd learned about those hands. When they had passed

185

through the last village, she had learned, She'd thought she could make her opportunity—he'd been lighting a cigarette—by seizing the wheel and trying to wreck the car, in the village there, where there were people to hear her screams.

But he'd struck her across the mouth with the back of his right hand, divining her plan before she'd put it into effect. The force of the blow had driven her into the corner. Her lower lip was cut against her teeth. There was blood in her mouth, and some of it had trickled down across her quivering chin.

He'd driven on, unhurried, matter-of-fact about it.

"You'd better wipe your face, baby," he'd told her in that quiet, even voice of his. And, defiantly, she hadn't. The blood was still there. The pain was still there, and the ache in her throat, and the smarting tears in her eyes.

She tried to fathom him, to dig out the purpose behind this snatch act he'd so coolly executed in broad daylight. She'd first laid eyes on him in the hallway of the lodging house where Alice Poynter had stayed.

Doro had got that far along a cold trail. She'd talked to Alice's landlady only to learn that Alice must have slipped away with bag and baggage in the small dark hours of Monday morning.

Doro had asked to use the 'phone that was situated in the hall. She'd called the *World*, was talking to Fairish when this young man with the obviously hennaed hair had stepped in through the open door. Doro had at first supposed he was one of the roomers.

And then, before the landlady could turn around, Duke had whipped out his gun for a swift blow to the head that had stretched the poor old woman on the floor at Doro's feet. He'd slammed the 'phone onto its stand, severing the connection. And Doro's scream had been cut short by the muzzle of Duke's gun driven deep into her side.

"Come on, baby, we're going places."

So they were going places at a dogged, steady forty miles an hour. She had thought him obviously a lamster, with his hair dyed like that. Her car with its press tag on the license plate had probably appealed to him as a means to avoid close attention from police. But if that was all, why hadn't he let her out somewhere along the line and gone off with the car?

That was only part of it, she decided—his getaway. But there was something else. Something that she knew?

She knew only that Jake Katz's picture and Alice Poynter's had been on cards in the same file in Miss Prudence's office. If that was what he was trying to keep quiet, he'd have his hands full, for she'd already relayed that much to Fairish. What was the significance? Why couldn't she grasp it?

She'd thought until her head ached, and she was exactly where she had begun—up against a blank wall. Against a bug-spattered windshield with a ribbon of road unwinding beneath relentlessly turning wheels.

THE SUN was low across the fields. The glare of it hurt her smarting eyes, blinded her at times. She wished that it would drop suddenly into the abyss beyond the horizon. No, not that. Not the dark. The glare was better—hold back the night.

Then he was slowing down. "Listen, baby," he said. "Get that blood off your mouth. I told you once, didn't I? I've got to stop for gas here, and I don't want nobody to get any ideas."

"I—I'll get it off," she said eagerly. Perhaps too eagerly for, as she scrubbed at her hurt mouth with her sodden handkerchief, she noticed the look he gave her.

Smile at him, her mind ordered. Go on. The old feminine charm. Give it to him—both barrels.

"Duke," she said and her smile quivered, "can I get out for a second up here at the station? Please, Duke. I've got to."

He looked at her, then back at the road. His soft mouth quirked.

"Sure, you can get out," he said. "For a second. You gotta powder your nose. Sure. Only—" he gestured with the gun—"remember."

"Yes. Yes, Duke."

"Not only you, see? The appleknocker who runs the station, too. One funny move, and I get both of you, see?"

"Yes, Duke."

"Just to the John," he said. "Get it? Nowhere else. If there's nobody around you could talk to, you can go."

Doro slid across the seat, under the wheel, and Duke took hold of her arm—a precautionary act, lest she try to start the car and make a break for it. She got out.

He kept that grip on her arm, conducted her to the corner of the building, nodded toward the entrance to the ladies' room, and released her. He and his gun watched her until the door had closed. Then he took a sidelong step to the coke cooler, opened it, and took out two bottles which he opened and put down on the top of the cooler.

He looked into the station office through the window. There was nobody there, and the aged attendant was busy at the pump. Duke took a small envelope from his pocket and poured two white pills out of its torn corner. These he dropped into the bottle on the left.

He took one bottle in each hand, moved back to the rear fender of the car. From there he could still watch the door of the ladies' room and yet talk to the station attendant.

"You and the missus off on a little vacation?" the old man asked.

Duke shook his head. "I wish we were," he said sadly. "No, I'm taking my wife to Chicago to the hospital."

The old man took the fill hose out of the tank opening and replaced the cap. He whipped a rag out of his rear pocket and shuffled up to wipe the windshield.

"She goin' to have an operation?" he asked sympathetically.

Duke shook his head. "Not that kind of a hospital." He tapped the center of his forehead suggestively.

"Oh."

"She's got what they call a persecution complex," Duke explained. "It hits her all of a sudden, and she's apt to start screaming for help or something like that." He put one of the bottles down carefully on the base of the pump and took a five dollar bill out of his pocket. "I just thought I'd mention that in case she does anything—well, peculiar."

THE OLD man took the bill. "You aim to drink the coke

here or take it with you? If you take it, you'll have to pay for the bottles."

"We'll take it." Duke turned his head toward the station and called, "Coming, honey?" And to the old man, "I may have to go after her. She sometimes gets the idea somebody is chasing her, and she'll lock herself in."

The old man counted change into Duke's hand. "Prosecution complex. That's a new one on me. I sure hope they cure her, Mister."

"So do I." Duke stuffed his change into his pocket, picked up the coke bottle, and started toward the door of the ladies' room. He'd reached the corner of the filling station when Doro appeared, walking slowly toward him, her eyes on his face, hating him.

Duke smiled, slightly, transferred the bottle to his left hand, slipped his right into the pocket where the gun was. He allowed her to pass and then fell in behind her, kept close to her as she climbed into the car.

"Here's your coke, honey."

"No thanks," she said icily. She slid under the wheel and as far to the right as possible. Duke got in and thrust one of the cold bottles into her hand.

"Take it," he ordered, his voice flat.

She glanced across at him. He hadn't touched his bottle. It was standing upright between his thighs, his right hand on the wheel, as before, his gun in the left.

Doro's hands clenched on the cold bottle. She was parched, but she didn't like the way he kept insisting that she drink.

Suppose he'd drugged the coke? She looked down longingly at the bottle and ran the quivering tip of her tongue along dry lips. She glanced at his bottle.

"Duke," she ventured, "if you'll trade bottles, I'll drink it. I'm awful thirsty."

He laughed. "Sure, baby. You think I poisoned it? Go ahead and trade."

She took his bottle, put it to her lips, and drank half of it without stopping.

"Why don't you drink yours?" she asked tauntingly when she paused for breath.

"I will later. Right now I'm not thirsty."

Doro made sounds like laughter. So he had put something in one of the cokes—in the bottle he had now. That was why he wasn't drinking. Assured, she raised her bottle again and finished the contents. She thought of the sign she had left in the rest room.

AM BEING KIDNAPED.
PHONE PENDLEVILLE WORLD
D. KELLY

She'd printed that in letters six inches high along one wall. She'd used the last inch of her lipstick to letter that plea in the station rest room.

Please, God, make him go in right away. Make him see the sign before it's too late. Before dark, make him see it.

She slumped in the seat and her head rolled back against the cushion. She closed her burning eyelids for a moment and thought rather laboriously that it was possible that Duke wasn't drinking because he couldn't manage the bottle, the gun, and the wheel at the same time.

It was suddenly of tremendous importance to her that he drink his coke. Why had he bought it if he didn't intend to drink it? And then the thought struck her that he *would* drink it—if she went to sleep.

When I go to sleep. But I mustn't. I won't let myself. He tricked me into asking for the coke that was drugged. He's clever and cruel, and he tricked me. But I won't go to sleep.

She raised her head a few inches, lifted heavy pricking eyelids a little way. The road was a gray satin ribbon that run on and on. The sun had dropped. The horizon ran with blood.

Doro Kelly's head fell back onto the cushions. The dark washed over her.

Duke Laymon glanced at the limp figure of the girl beside him. He grinned. Now he could drink his coke.

NED BARDON approached the door of his apartment at dusk. He was standing in the corridor, selecting the proper key, when the door swung slowly inward. Standing just across the threshold was a huge man in blue overalls and a grease-smeared denim cap. He was holding a small automatic pistol in an enormous left hand.

Ned Bardon's gaze traveled upward to the broad, fleshy face. Schoenling.

"Step in, please," Schoenling said dryly. "Fat Paul isn't the patient man he once was."

Ned Bardon entered the room. The room had another occupant—a short, swarthy individual, with small black eyes and cheeks that were pitted with pock marks, who sat in a straight chair to the right of the door. He too wore dirty overalls and a cap.

Ned Bardon looked back at Schoenling. "I get it," he said evenly in spite of the inner trembling that had taken hold of him. "It's a disguise. How did you two get in?"

"Picked the lock," Schoenling said. "Nick did," indicating the smaller man with a jerk of his head. "Nick Kalapolis. I don't think you've met."

They didn't shake hands.

"What did you do with those securities I left with you?" Schoenling demanded.

Ned Bardon said, "I told you it would take a little time, didn't I?"

Nick Kalapolis stood suddenly, and standing was a part of the blow that drove his right fist deep into Ned Bardon's lean middle. As Bardon doubled over, Nick brought up his knee to Bardon's chin. Bardon's head snapped back. He slid slowly down the door until he was sitting on the floor at Nick's feet.

Schoenling said, "Don't kill him."

"No, by geez. Just half kill him." Nick caught hold of Ned Bardon's lapels and hauled the blond man up onto his feet, kept him there with one hand braced against Bardon's chest. Bardon's head rocked to the left. Pink spittle trickled out of the side of his mouth. He mumbled something—a name for Nick Kalapolis.

"You've been working with Zero, haven't you? Him and the cops, you son!"

Bardon was shaking his head. "That's not true. Zero stole the securities. If he hadn't got them from me, he'd have got them from you. You can't beat something you can't see."

Schoenling sighed hugely. "Fat Paul has been awfully good to you, Bardon." He shook his head "But not anymore. Fat Paul is fresh out of patience. Come on, Nick."

Nick Kalapolis yanked Ned Bardon forward by the fullness of his coat, slammed a brass-knuckled fist into the side of Ned Bardon's head. Bardon was out on his feet, and Nick swung him around and let him fall in a heap beside the door.

Nick and Fat Paul went out into the corridor and closed the door behind them.

LEE ALLYN stumbled into the *World* city room at 10:05 P.M., his face drawn, his eyes haggard. Ordinarily there would have been no one there at this hour except the night man, but anxiety over Doro Kelly had kept Fairish and a few others at their posts. They all descended on Allyn now, the obvious question on their lips.

Allyn shook his head. "It's no good," he said tonelessly. "No damned good. I've been with the cops, and we've turned over every rat's nest in this town. They got Schoenling and a hood named Nick Kalapolis. Schoenling is in the hospital with about six police slugs in him, and they're working on Kalapolis now."

Fairish brightened somewhat. "That's something."

"But not enough. Kalapolis is small fry, and Schoenling may not live to talk. And—" Lee Allyn swallowed—"I just wrapped a *World* car around a lamp post. I'm so damned tired I'm seeing double."

194

Fairish threw an arm around the young man's slight shoulders. "The hell with that. Come on back here. I've got just what you need in my desk."

He didn't need anything except news that Doro Kelly was all right, but Lee Allyn permitted himself to be conducted to Fairish's desk where Fairish insisted upon him taking the chair. Fairish got out a pint bottle of good whiskey, uncorked it, and handed it to Allyn.

"You heard about old George Rumpler?" Allyn asked before tipping the bottle to his mouth.

Fairish nodded. "Off the teletype late this afternoon. Smothered in a fire somewhere up in the hills west of here."

"Maybe smothered, period," Allyn said. "The fire could have been just so much smoke screen. Rumpler was scheduled for murder."

The 'phone rang, and Lee Allyn's hand moved faster than any of the others that reached for the instrument.

"*World* city room," he said.

"One moment please," came from the receiver.

"It's long distance," Allyn said for the benefit of the others. "She's talking to the Rosedale operator now. Were you expecting anything, Fairish?"

Fairish was scowling, shaking his head. "Rosedale, Rosedale. Who in the hell do I know in Rosedale?" He turned suddenly and jabbed two fingers into the ribs of the gangling Wayland Pagget who let out a startled yip. "The Poynter girl, Wayland. Alice Poynter—wasn't she from Rosedale?"

"How would I know?" Pagget asked.

"You spent half your time talking to her."

"Shut up, can't you?" Allyn broke in. "I've got somebody here, and it isn't Alice Poynter. Hello, hello. What was that name again?"

A man's voice came faintly from the receiver. "Millsbaugh. M-i-l-l-s-b-a-u-g-h. Millsbaugh's Service Station twenty miles south of Rosedale. Is this the Pendleville *World?*"

"Yes, yes," Allyn said irritably. "You sure you don't want the circulation department?"

"I dunno," said the man on the other end of the line. "I don't know who I want, but there was a woman in my ladies' room this evenin', and her husband said she had a prosecution complex."

"A what?"

"Prosecution complex. It's a kind of craziness, he said. And she wrote all over the wall of my ladies' room with lipstick."

"Why tell us about it?" Allyn wanted to know. He looked up at Fairish and said, "Some crazy old coot—"

"Well, if she's crazy," came from the receiver, "that's all I want to know. Because that's what her husband said and I wasn't to pay no attention to what she did. But I didn't like his looks much, and I thought I'd find out if it was craziness or if she really was kidnaped."

"Hey, wait!" Allyn bounced forward in the chair. "Hang on a minute, old timer. Did you say kidnaped?"

"That's what I said, but if she's crazy, don't pay it no mind."

Allyn took a quivering breath. "Listen, Mr. Millsbaugh, we'll start all over. We'll start with what the lady wrote on the wall of the rest room."

"She wrote, 'Am being kidnaped.' Phone Pendleville *World*. D. Kelly.' But her husband said she was crazy, so—"

"And when was this?"

"Along about eight o'clock, I guess. I didn't get to clean the ladies' room until around half an hour ago, and I been tryin' to get you fellas since then."

"Eight o'clock," Allyn groaned. Over two hours ago, and Rosedale was over a hundred miles away. "Wait a minute, Mr. Millsbaugh. I'll let you talk to the editor."

"Then the lady ain't crazy, huh?"

"No, she isn't crazy." Allyn shoved the 'phone into Fairish's hands. "The guy has seen Doro. Get the details. Notify the state cops, the Rosedale cops—whatever you think best. I'm going to Rosedale."

As Allyn legged for the door of the city room, Wayland Pagget fell in beside him.

"In my car, Lee," Pagget insisted. "We'll take my car."

CHAPTER 17
A DATE WITH DEATH

AT 11:00 P.M. Wayland Pagget hoisted the aerial of his car radio and brought in Pendleville's station in the middle of a commercial.

"Turn that damned thing off," Lee Allyn said. For an instant he took his eye off the road and glanced at the speedometer. They were wrapped up sixty miles from the heart of Pendleville. Sixty lousy little miles, and it wasn't enough. By forty-eight miles, it wasn't enough. Now three full hours had elapsed since the filling station operator had seen Doro Kelly, and forty-eight miles meant nearly as many minutes.

Pagget hadn't turned the radio off. In fact, he boosted the volume above the throb of the engine and the rush of the air-stream through open windows.

"It'll take my mind off your driving," he said.

"You didn't have to come," Allyn snapped. "You could have—" He broke off as the voice of a news announcer came from the loudspeaker on the instrument panel.

Pendleville police have cracked the hot bond ring, according to Chief-of-Police Cavanaugh. Paul Schoenling, a pawn broker and alleged fence, together with Nick Kalapolis, a Jessop Street hoodlum, were surprised by police when the pair, posing as railroad section hands, attempted to board a west bound freight. Schoenling died at 10:35 in General Hospital of wounds received in the gun battle with police, and Kalapolis is being questioned by city police.

Another member of the Jessop Street mob whose name is slated for a return engagement in newspaper headlines tomorrow is Jake Katz, alias Robert Harbin. Katz is assumed to have been killed Sunday at midnight, although his body was not found until today.

An affidavit has been filed with the prosecuting attorney by Miss Madge Murphy of 1245 Franklin Street charging Ned Bardon, local securities dealer, with Katz's murder. According to Miss Murphy, Bardon, a former sweetheart, waylaid her and Katz when the couple was on the way home from a movie and beat Katz to death with a lug wrench. Police, up to the time of this broadcast, have not succeeded in locating Bardon.

"That's a frame," Lee Allyn inserted. "Bardon killed Katz, sure, but the whole thing is—"

"Shut up a minute," Pagget broke in, listening intently to the newscaster.

Still on Pendleville's crime front, State Police were alerted to be on the lookout for a gray Plymouth coupé owned by Doro Kelly, a reporter for the Pendleville World. The car is supposed to have been stolen by Duke Laymon, still another member of the Jessop Street mob, and it is assumed that Miss Kelly is being forced to accompany Laymon, and authorities were urged to proceed with caution on that account.

"These are all parts of the same jigsaw puzzle we have been trying to assemble," asserted Chief-of-Police Cavanaugh. "The mysterious deaths of four members of the Bachelors' Club, the Inland Street Branch Bank hold-up, the—"

Lee Allyn reached out and snapped off the radio switch. "All parts, maybe," he growled, "but you'll never put them together that way, Ed."

He gripped the wheel and swept the car into a wide curve. The big low-pressure tires screamed like banshees, and the badly frightened Wayland Pagget was thrown against Lee Allyn's right shoulder.

"Take it easy!" Pagget gasped as Allyn brought the car out of a flat spin. "You can't expect to keep this up all night. What makes you so sure the trail is going to end at Rosedale, anyway?"

"Alice Poynter. Her home town."

"But where does Alice fit in?"

ALLYN SHOOK his head. "I'm not sure, but I can make a

guess. I know that Ned Bardon didn't willfully kill Jake Katz. Katz was out with a girl that night. She ran to Bardon for help, and in the struggle, Bardon happened to kill Katz.

"Suppose it was Alice Poynter who was out with Jake Katz that night—not Madge Murphy. Madge's affidavit—a frame up—won't hold water if Alice talks. So Duke Laymon is heading for Rosedale to see that Alice doesn't talk. Duke Laymon is acting on orders from Schoenling. Duke probably doesn't know that Schoenling is all washed up, all of which isn't going to help Doro and Alice one damned bit. Have you got all that?"

"Well, yes," Pagget replied dubiously.

"Then start concentrating on one of Einstein's theories or on something simple like that, and let me drive."

Pagget braced his feet against the floorboards, his terrified eyes on the climbing needle of the speedometer. And Lee Allyn drove in tight-lipped silence, turning over and over again in his mind the few odd little pieces of the puzzle that still didn't fit anywhere. Little things, like a bottle of flat champagne.

"Pagget," Lee Allyn said after a moment, "what sort of a night was Sunday night?"

"Oh, hot," Pagget replied absently.

"Would you call it a pleasant night?"

"Huh uh. It was too hot and sticky. I couldn't sleep. That's why I was up until the small hours of the morning working on my Geiger counter."

That damned Geiger counter! Allyn thought.

He said, "Duncan Moore seemed to think Sunday night was all right. A nice evening."

"Maybe when you're as old as Duncan Moore was you can take a lot of heat," Pagget suggested. "But it was too hot for me. Why all this interest in last Sunday's weather?"

"Oh, just a little discrepancy I happened to recall. That and the flat champagne. Hey, did you notice that sign back there?"

"At this speed, which I estimate roughly as being supersonic, who can read signs? Anyway, who would want to?"

"I think it said ten miles to Rosedale. And I hope to God that when we get there, the Rosedale cops will have some news."

IT WAS 11:35 by the time they reached the outskirts of Rosedale, a town of perhaps eight thousand, and the sidewalks had been rolled up for at least an hour. It took fifteen precious minutes to locate the municipal building that housed fire and police departments.

Lee Allyn, terribly conscious of the approach of midnight, led the gangling Wayland Pagget into a basement office. There a cop with sergeants' chevrons on the sleeve of the coat he wasn't wearing, looked up from the pages of a magazine and grunted at them.

Allyn said, "We're from the Pendleville *World*. Got anything on our Miss Kelly yet?"

"Yup, we have."

It was impossible to tell from the man's exasperatingly slow manner of speaking whether what he had was good or bad. Allyn reeled slightly, and clutched the edge of the desk. "Good lord, have you found her or haven't you? Is she alive?"

"Well, I wouldn't know about that," replied the sergeant. "We got her car, though. Found it in a parking lot off Main Street. No bullet holes and no blood. We got it locked up in the department garage, if you want to see it."

Allyn put his hand up against the rays from the lamp on the desk. To the others it probably appeared to be only a nervous gesture, but the deepening aura of translucency at the finger tips told him of the swift approach of the zero hour. Once more he appealed to the cop behind the desk and his voice trembled.

"Alice Poynter—do you know where she is? Can you find out?"

"I guess she's home with her folks. Or then again she might be out with some boy. She's got lots of boy friends around."

Allyn turned in desperation to Wayland Pagget whose befuddled expression established him rather definitely as the last possible resort.

"Find out, can you, Pagget? Alice Poynter—you could telephone. I've got to find the men's room." And turning, he caught the indicative jerk of the sergeant's thumb and bolted through a door.

Wayland Pagget picked up the 'phone. He pushed the instrument into the sergeant's hands.

"You call her," he urged. "Alice Poynter. Ask where she is."

"Hate to get Sam Poynter out of bed at this hour. You're sure Alice is mixed up in this?"

Pagget ducked his head. "It—it's—" he waved his arms—"all very complicated. Alice knows too much. That is, she is slated for a rub-down, to resort to the vernacular."

"Slated for a what?"

"Somebody is going to kill her," Pagget said, blinking rapidly.

"You know—she might talk. At least that's Allyn's opinion, and he's very clever about murders."

"Hello," the sergeant said into the transmitter. "Sam? Well, say, Sam, this is Sergeant Meeker talking. Is Alice at home?… Oh?… Oh?… No, it's just that a man is here looking for her. He's from Pendleville. Some newspaper—"

There was someone there, waiting for Schoenling.

Pagget caught the sergeant's thick arm and shook it. "Where is she?" he stage-whispered.

"Okay, Sam. Sorry to disturb you at this hour. Good-bye." The sergeant put down the 'phone. "She's gone to the country club dance with the Clark boy. They expect her home about one. Which don't look to me like anything much to get alarmed about. Ronny Clark is a nice boy."

Pagget turned away from the desk, crossed to the door through which Allyn had presumably entered the men's room. Pagget knocked.

"Lee, she's at the country club dance," Pagget said.

There was no answer. Pagget looked blankly at the police sergeant.

"Do you suppose he's fainted, or something?"

"Open the door and find out."

"Yes, of course." Pagget seized the knob, twisted it, and came close to bumping his nose on the unyielding panel. The door was bolted on the inside, and Pagget's repeated knocking remained unanswered.

Outside the police station, a car started up.

ALICE POYNTER paused for a glance at herself in the powder room mirror at the Rosedale Country Club. Her soft young mouth curved in a smile. She was rather pleased with the way she looked tonight, bare shoulders blossoming from frothy pink chiffon, her blond hair in the new Mary Martin bob.

Not beautiful, as Ronny Clark had told her she was, a few minutes earlier. Not sophisticated looking. Admittedly a small town girl, not career minded. Not since last Sunday night had she been career minded.

Mirror dark, mirror bright, she thought, show me the one I love tonight.

Pulse quickening, her step light, Alice left the powder room to enter the softly lighted ballroom. Near the entrance were two men who were looking at her—Luther Danberry and a stranger wearing a neat brown suit and a straw snap-brim. They exchanged a word, inaudible above the music of the band, and then the stranger hurriedly cut across a corner of the floor to intercept Alice.

"Miss Poynter, I believe."

Alice paused. He'd taken off his hat, and his hair was a true mahogany color. His face was smooth, inclined toward fleshiness.

"My name is Brown," he said. "You don't know me, and I'm very sorry to intrude in this way, but this is very important."

"Yes?" Alice said, her manner restrained. There was something about this Mr. Brown she did not like. Nothing that she could put her finger on, but there was something—something not quite right about him.

He took her arm impersonally and led her to the edge of the dance floor. "You know a Miss Doro Kelly of Pendleville?" he asked. "I believe she's employed by the *World*."

"Yes," Alice replied. The snooty Kelly person, she remembered. She remembered her well.

"Miss Kelly has been suddenly taken ill," Mr. Brown explained. She asked me to look you up—she doesn't know anyone else in Rosedale. I have her outside with me in the car right now. I wonder if you'd just step out and talk to her a moment."

"Why—why—" Alice stammered—"I suppose so." Whether she supposed so or not, she found herself being led through the door and out onto the broad veranda. Fear nudged her and passed on. The glow of cigarettes along the veranda rail, the young laughter reassured her. Nothing could happen here. She oughtn't to let first impressions influence her.

"Were you just passing through Rosedale?" she asked Mr. Brown as they hurried together across the broad parking area.

"Yes. This Miss Kelly had some trouble with her car, a few miles south of here, and I gave her lift. She doesn't seem at all well." Mr. Brown sidled between cars with Alice in tow, opened the rear door of a battered black sedan, and turned on a flashlight.

DORO KELLY was curled up on the back seat cushions, her eyes closed. She appeared very pale in the light beam, and her breathing was heavy, labored. Alice Poynter uttered a small, compassionate cry and immediately got into the car to crouch on the floor. She raised the unconscious girl to a sitting position.

"Miss-Kelly!" Alice shook the other girl. "Wake up, Miss Kelly."

Miss Kelly moaned, but didn't open her eyes. Alice sent a wild-eyed glance over her shoulder at Mr. Brown.

"We'll have to get her to the hospital right away."

"Okay," Brown agreed, "but you'll have to tell me how to get there."

"Out the main drive and turn to your right," Alice replied. "But hurry."

"Just as fast as I can make it," Brown said. He shot forward in second, snapped into high, and took the curve onto the highway fast enough to burn rubber.

Doro Kelly moaned softly and Alice help-lessly patted the other girl's shoulder.

Alice Poynter

"You poor, poor child, you," Alice whispered sympathetically. "Everything is going to be all right. It's Alice, honey. Alice Poynter, remember?"

"Alice," Doro repeated dazedly. "Sweet Alice, the Daring Girl Reporter. Got to find Sweet Alice."

"I'm right here, honey. Everything's all right—"

And suddenly Alice realized that everything was all wrong. The car had braked at the side of the road, and it was the wrong road—a narrow lane with a wooded thicket on the right side.

She saw Mr. Brown bound across the front seat to get out on the right hand side, to open the door of the rear compartment. The ray of his flashlight blinded her and limned Doro Kelly's pale face and glazed eyes. It glinted on steel that jutted from Mr. Brown's hand. A gun. No doubt about it. A gun.

Alice Poynter screamed.

"This," said Duke Laymon, as his finger tightened on the trigger, "is it."

It might have been a gust of wind that rattled the branches along the side of the car. As sudden as that, as unseen. It struck Duke Laymon with hurricane force, caught his gun arm, deflected it.

It twisted and tripped the gunman so that he went crashing down into the brush. The way the branches thrashed, Duke Laymon might have been having an epileptic seizure. And then—silence unbroken except by someone's heavy breathing.

The flashlight was still burning down there somewhere in the weeds. Doro's staring eyes saw it turn and lift, watched it point down at the still figure in the neat brown suit at the side of the road. Then the flashlight floated through the open door of the car, showed her Alice Poynter in a dead faint, her blond head back against the cushions.

"You're all right, angel?"

The unmistakable voice of Captain Zero. Doro Kelly tipped forward on the seat cushion. Invisible arms that were warm and strong closed about her.

"All right," she whispered. She closed her eyes, tips of her fingers caressing the face she could not see. It was like being blind and loving someone you would never see. His kiss was warm and searching.

Then he was speaking to her in quiet urgency.

"We've got to get back to Pendleville. This car or any car. But we've got to get back. Have to take Alice with us."

"And—Duke?" Doro ventured.

"He can stay here. Forever. I'm afraid I was a bit too violent with Duke. Lost my temper. But when I saw you in the car back there at the country club—"

"Country club? Where are we?" She hadn't opened her eyes. Too infrequently the arms of Captain Zero held her thus, and she meant to make it last.

"Rosedale," he said. *"Just outside the town. I intercepted you at the club, rode out here on the front bumper."* He sighed. *"Too bad, angel, but we've got to get moving. I've got a date with a murderer."*

CHAPTER 18
THE NOOSE HANGS HIGH

MISS ADA FRANZER awoke with a start from a nightmare about a noose. It was—or rather had been—a noose of fine and incredibly strong silk thread, and someone had looped it over her head to tighten it from behind.

She sat up, gasping, and her fingers sought the soft, unblemished flesh of her throat. And then, remembering, her eyes darted to the east window.

It was still there—that nooselike silhouette projected on the curtain. Just a raveling, or something of the sort, that hung down from the valance of the awning, Miss Ada Franzer told herself, and it was perfectly ridiculous to let a little thing like that upset you.

And then, as she stared at the shadow of the miniature noose, it moved. It didn't sway as though in the wind, for there wasn't any wind. It moved gradually upward, crawled behind the valance of the awning, and disappeared.

Miss Ada Franzer was not given to screaming. For one so long out of practice, she did a rather creditable job of it. She screamed and bounded out of the bed, backed away from the window, and sidled to the bedroom door where her fumbling fingers found the light switch and got it on.

She didn't pause there, but went on into the living room, barefooted and in her pink nightgown, to turn on every single light she could lay her hands on.

Basil-the-clock informed her that the time was 3:47 A.M. Miss Franzer goggled at the familiar surroundings as though she'd never seen them before.

"I've got to do something," she said aloud and wrung her hands.

She had to do something because, for the second time, something was wrong upstairs. Duncan Moore's apartment was vacant. Yet *somebody* was up there. Somebody was up there to remove that little noose of thread from the awning. Which could mean only one thing: the noose wasn't a raveling, a thing of chance—it was a clue. Something the murderer didn't want found and understood.

Miss Franzer's mind took a backward lurch to Sunday night. She'd been lowering the awning at her accustomed time when the volley of gunfire had broken out in the room above.

"And that little noose—" Miss Franzer put both hands up to her throat as though the noose were actually about her own throat. "Gracious!" she gasped and, her heart thumping in her throat, she padded across the living room to the telephone.

She was on the verge of picking up the instrument when small frantic fists beat on her front door. Miss Franzer turned and goggled at the door.

"Ada!" somebody stage-whispered from the other side of the panel. "Ada, for heaven's sake, let me in!"

Miss Franzer crossed to the door without further hesitation, unlocked it, and opened it. Ann Gerard, wearing a spicy brown eyelet dress, white gloves but no hat, came into the room.

"Heavens, darling!" Miss Franzer caught Ann by both arms. "I never was so glad to see anyone in my life."

"Really?" Ann broke away and closed the door behind her.

"You know that little noose that kept me awake last night?" Miss Franzer was saying. "I told you at luncheon, remember? Something has just happened to it. Someone is upstairs—where there oughtn't to be anybody—and that someone has removed the little noose of thread."

Ann appeared concerned. "You've called the police?"

"No, not yet. I was just about to. It's a clue, I know it is. Look, darling, you know how I lower that awning every night. I'm quite punctual about it."

"Yes, you are," Ann said evenly. She was opening the clasp of her brown purse. "You're in a terrible nit, Ada."

"Well, suppose that little piece of thread attached to my awning extended up through the screen of Duncan Moore's window directly above," Miss Franzer speculated excitedly. "And suppose that little noose were attached to something—something like—"

"Something like this?" Ann said, smiling oddly. She brought a tiny flat automatic pistol out of her purse.

"Well, I was thinking of that other thing. That shooting device, scare gun, or what—" Miss Franzer goggled at the little gun in Ann's hand. "Gracious, child, where did you get that?"

"It isn't a scare gun," Ann said quietly. "Though you're quite right about the other time when it *was* a scare gun. You're terribly right, Ada, I'm very sorry to say."

And then she pointed the little automatic much as she might have pointed a finger. She pointed it at the bosomy figure in the pink nightgown and pulled the trigger.

MINUTES LATER, as she was running up the steps to her own apartment, it occurred to her that there was another danger—the gun in her purse. She ought to get rid of that. The gun, the piece of thread with the fish-hook attached, and the phonograph record. Three things.

She unlocked the door of her apartment, switched on the living room lamps, and hurried into the adjoining bedroom. There she opened her purse, took out the gun, the bit of thread with the hook attached, and put these two items down on her dresser. She put the purse on the bed, moved to the closet, and brought out her own traveling case and the brown masculine looking satchel that contained the money.

She flung the traveling case on the bed, opened it, and then raced to the chest of drawers. She paused, lips apart, a worried frown on her beautiful face. The record, she thought. She'd better put the record with the other two items that had to be got rid of. And she'd better do it right now.

She went back into the living room and approached the lamp table that stood at the right end of the sofa. She lifted the lamp, her fingers going to the base of it. Her face was frozen into a mask of stark fear as she stared down at a green circular piece of felt that lay on the surface of the table where the lamp had stood. Someone had removed that felt pad from the lamp base.

The record was gone.

Ann's terrified gaze swept across the room, into the vestibule, to the door. The metallic sound was distinctly that of a key being inserted in the lock. The knob turned. Ann let the lamp fall from nerveless fingers. It struck the table, toppled, crashed to the floor.

The door opened and Ned Bardon stepped into the apartment.

Ann drew a deep, relieved breath, flew across the room, and threw herself into Ned's arms.

"My darling," she sobbed. "Oh, my darling. I didn't know—I thought—" But why talk now?

They kissed passionately, and then Ann had to know why he was here instead of in that tourist cabin where he had planned to hide; where she would have gone to meet him before they headed south.

Ned Bardon said, "The police found me shortly after midnight. I've been down at the station until about half an hour ago."

She stared at his face. "The police?" she repeated faintly. "They let you go?"

He nodded, laughing. "Captain Zero pulled a chestnut out of the fire for me. I had a notion he would if I stuck to him long enough. He turned up with the girl Jake Katz was really out with Sunday night. Not Madge—some girl by the name of Poynter."

He shrugged, "I'm a free man. Madge will have to face a perjury charge. My alibi is considerably stronger than ever, and we can be married here and then go to South America at

Lee Allyn

our leisure, or we can go tonight and be married on shipboard. Whatever you say, sweetheart."

Ann's face was very grave. Ned Bardon glanced away from it a moment and to the lamp on the floor.

"What gives with the lamp?" he asked. "Not artistic temperament, surely."

"The record, Ned. It's gone."

His smile faded. His face was suddenly pale, waxlike. "Gone? I thought you destroyed it."

SHE WAS shaking her head. "I should have. I told you I did.

But then I didn't. Because I love you so, Ned. Because I always want to keep you, I kept the record."

"I see," he said slowly. "Something you could hold over me."

"Only to hold you to me darling, for always. But—" she drew, a nervous fluttering gesture—"it's gone. And that isn't all. I killed Ada Franzer."

Ned Bardon caught her arms. His eyes locked with hers.

"You—what?"

"I killed Ada Franzer," she repeated. "Just now. I had to. She told me at noon about the piece of thread. I got the key to the Moore apartment from Manuel tonight and went there to get the thread off the awning. And I heard Ada's scream. I *had* to, darling—don't look at me like that.

"I had to kill her because she'd guessed that when she let her awning fall Sunday night, the loop of thread had pulled the trigger on Duncan Moore's scare gun. She was going to call the police. Don't you see, if she'd opened her mouth to them, your alibi would have been broken."

He said tonelessly. "You killed her." He broke off, his head tipped somewhat to the right, listening.

Ann heard it too. A faint hum. It came from the chairside radio-phonograph combination on the other side of the room. And then, from the loudspeaker came a voice. An old man's voice. A dead man's voice.

"Lovely weather we're having, isn't it?" said the voice of Duncan Moore from the phonograph, "Not too warm, not too cool."

There was a pause. Ned Bardon and Ann Gerard stood rooted to the spot.

"Well," said the voice, "good night, Bardon."

Ned Bardon snarled. His right hand streaked to the side pocket of his coat. He was immediately aware that there was another hand quicker than his—a hand that had dipped into that same pocket.

Ned Bardon whirled, found himself looking into the muzzle of his own silencer-fitted weapon. That it seemed suspended in thin air with no visible means of support made it no less threatening, for the hand that held it was Captain Zero's.

"What, you didn't think to double-check with a Geiger counter?" Zero asked mockingly. *"No, no, Ann—"* as the girl took a step nearer Ned Bardon. *"You two have done very well together, and I intend to keep you apart."*

Ned Bardon said, "Ann hasn't had anything to do with it."

"No?" Zero said dubiously. *"Who made the plates for the spurious Reynox stock certificates that you used to con Moffet, McAlister, Duncan Moore, and George Rumpler? Miss Gerard told me she had had some experience with etchings. You know, that's what has made you two so difficult to catch. You've been so utterly truthful.*

"When I noticed the scraps of felt in Miss Gerard's wastebasket, she coolly told me she had been making a new base pad for that lamp. So I hadn't the slightest difficulty finding the phonograph record—the lamp base made an admirable hiding place, my dear—once I decided that it had to be a record."

"What made you so damned sure it was?" Ned Bardon wanted to know. "There was no phonograph in Duncan Moore's library."

"*The discrepancy about the weather. Sunday night was hot and humid and thoroughly uncomfortable.*

"*Cavanaugh asked what you were talking about, and Manuel said you were saying how nice the weather was.*

"*When I first visited your apartment, there was small phonograph disk on your radio record player. Your radio record player, I repeat. That record was a love message from a girl to her G.I. sweetheart. But you thought it was the incriminating record, didn't you? You were obviously relieved when Madge's voice—not Duncan Moore's—came from the reproducer. I wondered why would a man in love with so charming a girl as Miss Gerard, here, be playing a recording from Madge Murphy?*

"**THE ANSWER,** *of course, is that Miss Gerard switched records before leaving your apartment.*

"*As to how the record of Duncan Moore's voice could be heard in Duncan Moore's library when there was no phonograph there, that's one of the more readily answered questions. The library contained a radio. Radio record players, such as you have, Bardon, are actually tiny broadcasting stations.*

"*Any good radio within the distance of a block has a chance to pick up music from a neighbor's radio record player. I presume you made that recording at some time previous when Duncan Moore visited your apartment?*"

Ned Bardon said, "I'm damned if I'll tell you anything."

Zero laughed quietly. "*So you've stopped being frank. You no longer believe honesty is the best policy. No matter. We can find out. You probably had a recording device sent out to your place on approval, especially to get a recording of Duncan Moore's voice as you said good-bye. Your own responses you would have had to edit out of the original record. It's too bad you couldn't have looked ahead at the weather situation, isn't it? You just might have got away with it."*

Ann Gerard said defiantly. "You still don't know anything. You're guessing, that's all."

"And guessing accurately," Zero went on coolly. *"I'll construct the whole crime for you now, including the other odd little item—the flat champagne. You two worked it together, and it was timed to a hair.*

The silencer-fitted muzzle
seemed suspended in the air.

*Ann was in your apartment, Bardon, ready with the radio record
player and the recording of Duncan Moore's farewell.*

*"You, Bardon, were in Moore's apartment. You had brought, as a
gift, a bottle of champagne which turned out to be so flat that nobody*

drank it. I'll venture to say you previously opened that bottle and let it get flat, then corked it again. The object being, of course, that when the bottle was opened at Moore's apartment there would be no characteristic pop.

"There could be only one pop without arousing Manuel's suspicion. If he heard one pop, he would conclude that you had opened the champagne. Actually, if he heard the pop at all, it came from this silenced gun I am holding in my hand right now.

"Because, Bardon," the voice of Zero went on, *"Duncan Moore was dead when you left his apartment. The radio record player in your apartment across the alley, the radio in Duncan Moore's library, provided the dead man with a voice. You coolly filled in your part of the farewell conversation with Manuel standing right beside you. It was then about eleven-forty.*

"You had to rig up Duncan Moore's scare gun in such a manner that it would go off when you were far, far away and thus falsify the time of death. You put a loop of thread on the trigger of that automatic shooting device, tied a hook of some sort to the end of that thread, dropped the thread out the window and engaged the hook in the canvas of the furled awning over the window of Miss Franzer's apartment below.

"Knowing that Miss Franzer was punctual about lowering her awning—here again you had Miss Gerard's help—you could rest assured that the scare gun would go off at midnight or very close to it. You would have an alibi for midnight. The bowling alley on Jessop Street."

Zero was aware of footsteps in the corridor outside. He called, "Come in, Cavanaugh. I've unlocked the door."

Ned Bardon took a lurching step toward Captain Zero, stopped as the gun moved an inch or so nearer. Ned Bardon looked at Ann Gerard hopelessly.

The door opened and Ed Cavanaugh came into the room alone. He had a pair of handcuffs ready, and when he saw that wasn't going to be enough, he brought out a set for Ann.

He said to anybody, "Miss Franzer isn't hurt badly. They tell me she's already named Miss Gerard." He snapped the bracelets on Ann Gerard's wrists, and she stood there, staring at them with glazed and unbelieving eyes.

Cavanaugh turned to Ned Bardon. "This is something I've been wanting to do for a long time," the chief said grimly as he clamped the cuffs on Bardon's wrists.

"*That's right,*" Zero said. "*Your hunch was good all the way through. What threw me off, of course, was Bardon's position as dupe for Schoenling. I knew, Cavanaugh, and you didn't. I knew Schoenling had that hold on Bardon. It was inconceivable then that Bardon was also Schoenling's boss, The Man in Black. And yet—he was.*"

Bardon laughed harshly. "That was the biggest kick I got out of it—muscling in on Fat Paul when he thought he had me under his heel."

Cavanaugh said, "But you did need Schoenling's Jessop Street mob to crack the bank and get those phony securities you'd peddled to Duncan Moore. After that, you didn't give a damn what happened to the Jessop Street boys. They made dandy red herrings to pitch at us while you went on about your business—which included smothering George Rumpler."

"You'll never prove that," Bardon said with a note of pride in his voice.

"Who has to prove it?" Cavanaugh asked. "Who has to prove that you killed Moffet and McAlister either, now that Zero has cracked your alibi and pinned the Duncan Moore job on you?"

"Yes, Bardon," Zero said, *"you only hang once. And you will."*